A Pilgrim's Notebook

Guide to Western Wildlife

dedication

*For a crusty old Desert Rat named Edward Abbey
who doesn't like much of anything—and says so—
but who, in his own, peculiar way, is one of America's
most verbal defenders of wildlife and wildland.*

A Pilgrim's Notebook

Guide to Western Wildlife

by Buddy Mays
with photographs by the author

 Chronicle Books/San Francisco

Chronicle Books
870 Market Street
San Francisco, CA 94102
(415) 777-7240

Library of Congress Cataloging in Publication Data

Mays, Buddy.
    A pilgrim's notebook,
        guide to western wildlife.

    Bibliography: p.
    Includes index.
    1. Zoology—The West.   I. Title.
QL155.M39   596'.0978   77-22043
ISBN 0-87701-103-6

Design by Brenton Beck
Illustration by Pedro Gonzalez
Fifth Street Design Associates

Composition by Hansen &
Associates Graphics

Printed in the United States of America

PREFACE

This book is a layman's guide, created especially for those who wish to observe, enjoy, and help conserve one of America's most valuable natural resources—wild animals. It is written for backpackers, hikers, canoeists, camp counselors, teachers, bird watchers, beginning naturalists, environmentalists, nature-loving children and their parents, hangglider pilots, boaters, sailors, and anyone else who might want to know more about wild animals, and is meant to be carried into the field in backpack, rucksack, or plain paper bag, not left behind on some dusty library shelf. Many of the terms used to describe certain aspects of animal behavior, though technically accurate, have been simplified for easier understanding.

The sheer magnitude of individual animal species that may be encountered by field observers makes it impossible to list them all. Instead, this book encompasses three general categories: those species that are common, those of exceptional interest, and those endangered or threatened with extinction. The task of choosing these individual species was made extremely difficult because of fluctuating regional populations, annual migrations (during which many species move en masse from one region to another), and the varied opinions of experts from whom I sought information. However, after long hours of discussion with other naturalists and geographical biologists, I have settled on the animals included here as those that best meet these criteria.

There are exceptions. For example, the wide range of small field and forest songbirds, though both common and interesting, was not included primarily because of space. Volumes of material have been written about the LGBs (Little Gray Birds), and yet more could be said. The same is true for most of the reptiles, though I have discussed rattlesnakes, several species of commonly encountered lizards, and the non-venomous snakes seen most frequently by humans. Nocturnal rats and mice, and a few of the larger nocturnal mammals, were left out because they usually go unnoticed by man. The night-active species I have included are those that sometimes, if not commonly, venture out in daylight, usually during late afternoon or at dusk. America's endangered or threatened animals are included simply to inform readers of their existence and struggle for precious survival. Most can be observed in the wild. However, the very rarest ones, like the black-footed ferret, the whooping crane, and a few others, have been omitted, since there is almost no chance that the amateur naturalist will ever see them.

Where possible, the discussion of each animal is accompanied by a photograph to assist in identification. Ninety percent of these pictures were shot in the wild—the product of long, enjoyable hours afield with camera, a bag of lenses, and lots of patience. In a few cases, however, it was necessary to photograph in zoological gardens, since some species are reluctant to allow humans to approach within camera range.

For the purpose of describing geographical range and habitat, I have assumed that the American West includes only the 11 traditional western states —Washington, Oregon, California, Arizona, Nevada, Utah, Idaho, Montana, Wyoming, Colorado, and New Mexico. However, since the range of many animals extends to Mexico, the two western provinces of Canada, Alaska, Texas, and the Dakotas, these outlying areas are also listed when individual species are commonly observed there.

The Glossary of Animal Tracks and the Glossary of Animal Skulls are intended to recreate track and skull characteristics as they should appear. Of course, many things—terrain, injury, even the animal's speed —can vary track and skull patterns, and these variances should be allowed for by the observer. In addition, the tracks and skulls of some species are rarely seen, usually because of their habitat. Consequently they are not listed in the glossaries.

Buddy Mays
June 1977

ACKNOWLEDGEMENTS

Special thanks to Tom Smylie, Public Information Officer, United States Fish and Wildlife Service, Southwest Region; Mr. Michael Williamson, curator of reptiles and birds, Rio Grande Zoological Park, Albuquerque, New Mexico; the United States Forest Service, Ghost Ranch Museum and Zoological Park; the California Humane Association at Monterey; and the Bigfoot Information Center, The Dalles, Oregon.

I am grateful to Mr. Henry Gibson for the use of his poem, "Appendix IV," and to Ft. Lewis College in Durango, Colorado, which readily lent me its mammal skull collection.

And a very special thanks to Mark Rosacker and Dean Ricer of the Living Desert State Park, Carlsbad, New Mexico.

A Pilgrim's Notebook

Guide to Western Wildlife

3/LARGE MAMMALS

4/AQUATIC MAMMALS

5/PRIMATES

INTRODUCTION

The rudiments of vertebrate life began on this planet we casually call Earth more than 400 million years ago, during a period scientists know as the Paleozoic era. Since that time, hundreds of thousands of vertebrate life forms have evolved. Some died out immediately because of a physical makeup unsuited for survival. Others, like the dinosaurs, lived on for millions of years, only to disappear when their molecular structures were unable to keep pace with a rapidly changing environment. Still others, those capable of making many minute adjustments in their physiological composition, remain with us today.

The first practical examination of these wildlife forms is relatively recent, at least when compared to the beginnings of life itself. Pictographs discovered in Italy, France, and Czechoslovakia, and estimated to be 40,000 years old, reveal that early man had a surprising knowledge of animal musculature. Pithecanthropus erectus, Neanderthal man, Cro-Magnon man, and others were fully versed in vertebrate behavioral patterns, since their daily survival depended on knowing enough about their fellow creatures to kill them with rock and spear. To early man's credit, he killed only what he could eat.

The first serious naturalists were the Greeks. Xenophanes, an observer of the 6th century B.C., was one of the first to recognize that fossils were actually animal remains, and to hint that fossils indicated that Greece had once been sea bottom. In the 3rd century B.C. Aristotle also wrote and lectured about zoology. His *Historia Animalium* is probably the first field guide to native animals of Greece and Asia. It was Aristotle who voiced the opinions that bees could and did produce young without benefit of sperm and that the higher life forms had evolved from lower ones.

For the next 2,000 years, however, very little was accomplished in the field of wildlife science or applied animal knowledge. The Romans, for example, victorious though they were in battle, did little except to compile information already known. Scholars in succeeding centuries read and studied these compilations but added little themselves to man's understanding of the animal world. Then, in 1735, the Swedish scientist Carolus Linnaeus published the first organized catalogue that grouped animals, plants, and minerals with common characteristics together. To each organism or item he gave a scientific name, and it is this major classification system that we still use in part today. Though it was more than a century later when Charles Darwin published *The Origin of the Species*, Darwin's work was only a finishing, if dramatic, touch to the knowledge that Linnaeus, Aristotle, Xenophanes, and others had already compiled.

It must be understood that until Darwin's time, world wildlife populations had followed their individual patterns of survival, unmolested for the most part except when killed for food. This was especially true in western North America, where an abundance of wildlife in thousands of different ecosystems existed with no other controls than those of nature herself. When a particular life form threatened the survival of other life forms (or itself) because of overpopulation, natural controls like scarce food supplies, predators, and in some species instinctive survival mechanisms took over and stabilized the system. Certainly animals were studied —mainly by Indians—but like primitive man before them, Indian hunters seldom killed more than they needed to fill the bellies of their families. They were, in fact, just another element in a natural system of control that had worked well for millions of years.

But from 1800 until early in this century, western America's wildlife faced a danger far greater than that of any predator ever known before. As man began a massive westward migration from the overpopulated East in search of land, wealth, and opportunity, the basic facts of natural selection, adaptation, and ecosystem control were forgotten or ignored. The knowledge of the Indians, Darwin, Linnaeus, even the cave men, meant little. Wild animals were considered pests and competitors, to be obliterated as efficiently as possible.

Early in the 20th century, when the final count was made, 50 million bison, 100 million pronghorns, and uncountable numbers of wild turkeys, deer, bears, wolves, coyotes, foxes, elk, beavers, waterfowl, and wild horses had fallen to the rifle or trap. Millions more of various species had starved to death after being driven from their traditional range. Hundreds of species were teetering on the brink of extinction, and more than 40 had gone over the edge.

Fortunately, however, by 1920, dedicated groups of men and women, working long hours without pay, had pushed legislation through Congress which protected many of America's wild animals. Consequently, some life forms were slowly nudged away from the threat of extermination and their populations once again stabilized. But it seems that man has learned nothing from what historians call the "Great American Slaughter." Western America's wildlife populations —and the populations of the world, in fact—are steadily declining, the result of an apparently irrepressible human impulse to destroy everything natural. Examples are commonplace. Almost every major waterway in the world, for instance, has been dammed at least once, with the resulting deadwater lakes destroying habitat, scenery, and in some cases, the migration patterns of fish. Waging war on carnivorous predators is now accepted practice in ranching and farming communities; and in most cases the animals are being

killed because of human ignorance. Eagles, for instance, shot or poisoned by the thousands each year, are mistakenly thought to prey heavily on domestic livestock, when in reality their dinner usually consists of field mice, jackrabbits, or dead fish. Similarly, the coyote has been totally extirpated in some areas for the same reason, when he is probably the most effective rodent control in the American West. Foxes, badgers, hawks, owls— the list is endless.

Through years of trial and error, environmentalists have found that public pressure is the most effective way to deal with problems like the one American wildlife is facing today. The nation's dwindling herd of bison, at one time numbering less than 100, was saved by an outcry so loud that it resounded in the White House itself. More recently, an enraged public, demanding protection for rare and endangered animals, helped pressure the Congress into passing the Endangered Species Act, a bill that without

help from concerned citizens might never have become law.

The key to public concern, of course, is information. *A Pilgrim's Notebook* is a compilation—as accurate as I can make it—of 15 years of personal field observation and the latest information published concerning the status of particular wildlife species found in western America. I hope this material will spur the reader to further thought and research, for it will be a prepared public, fully aware of the aesthetic and physical value of animals other than ourselves, who will eventually save our wildlife if such is to be its fate.

APPENDIX IV

Strange that man should make up lists
Of living things in danger
Why he fails to list himself
Is really even stranger.

Henry Gibson

1/ SMALL MAMMALS

Kangaroo Rats

IDENTIFICATION

Generally, the 16 species of kangaroo rat found in the western United States are similar in appearance. Their basic body color is grayish-brown with white underparts. The hind legs are large and muscular. The tail, usually dark, tufted on the end, and striped with white on both sides, is always longer than the head and body combined. Kangaroo rats have large, friendly black eyes, short ears, and extremely long salt-and-pepper whiskers. The three most common western varieties are described below, but because of their nocturnal habits, identifying individual species in the field is difficult.

Ord's Kangaroo Rat (*Dipodomys ordii*). 9-10 inches long, including a 6-inch tail. *There are usually five toes on the hind foot.* Found throughout the western states except in Washington, western California, western Oregon, and the western half of Montana.

Ord's Kangaroo Rat

Merriam's Kangaroo Rat (*Dipodomys merriami*). 9 inches long, including a 5-inch tail. *There are usually four toes on the hind foot.* Found in New Mexico, Arizona, Nevada, Utah, and California, and rarely in Texas.

Merriam's Kangaroo Rat

Banner-Tailed Kangaroo Rat (*Dipodomys spectabilis*). A very large rat, 12-15 inches long, including a 9-inch tail. The tail tuft is black *with a white spot at the end.* Found in western Texas, southern New Mexico, and southeastern Arizona.

Banner-Tailed Kangaroo Rat

HABITAT

Kangaroo rats prefer brushy, arid desert or high grassland with plenty of sandy soil available. They are hole dwellers residing either in single-family burrows with two or more entrances (Ord's and Merriam's) or in large, honeycombed mounds with up to 70 feet of intricate, spacious tunnels (banner-tailed).

VOICE

Seldom heard unless the animals are kept as pets. A purr or growl when angry or in pain; a squeak when frightened.

FOOD

Wild seeds, beans, grain, and grasses. Like most small rodents, kangaroo rats often hoard food inside their burrows in bushel quantities. Food is gathered each night, carried in the rat's cheek pouches to a shallow hole, covered with sand, and allowed to cure in the following day's sunlight before being stored in the tunnel.

ENEMIES

Kangaroo rats are a primary source of protein for almost all desert-dwelling carnivorous birds, mammals, and reptiles. Their most dangerous foes are nocturnal owls and rattlesnakes; the latter can pursue them into their burrows.

STATUS

Inhabiting a small range in southern California, the Morro Bay kangaroo rat is officially listed as an Endangered Species. Other species are common. In certain areas where coyote, rattlesnake, and predator bird populations have been destroyed, kangaroo rat populations have reached pest levels.

THINGS YOU SHOULD KNOW

Very adept at water conservation, kangaroo rats remain underground during the day in their cool burrows, protected from the sunlight by several feet of earth. They venture above ground at or shortly after sundown to feed until driven back underground by cool mornings or predators. Perhaps their

Kangaroo Rat (male)

most unusual characteristic is a unique metabolism which absorbs moisture from digesting food and returns it to their system. Consequently they never sweat, and their feces and urine contain only minute amounts of moisture. Normally kangaroo rats go through life without ever taking a drink of water.

Solitary animals, they usually live by themselves except during mating season. Their only defense against predators is speedy and erratic flight in the form of 6-foot leaps. Sometimes, however, when confronted with suspicious objects, they may use their hind feet as shovels, spraying sand in the object's "face" and escaping in the resulting confusion.

With the exception of the banner-tailed variety, which can seldom be tamed, kangaroo rats make excellent pets when kept in a closed environment like an aquarium partially filled with sand. They survive well on a diet of oatmeal and lettuce, are not smelly, and seldom if ever bite.

Woodrats

ALIAS
Packrat, Cave-Rat, Trade-Rat.

IDENTIFICATION
Most western varieties of woodrat are similar in appearance. They are large, grayish-brown rodents with furry ears, long, silky fur, and slender, round tails. Individual species are generally distinguished by size, tail structure, and the location where they are found.

White-Throated Woodrat (Neotoma albigula). 13-16 inches long, including a 7-inch tail. The tail is distinctive—dark above and white below, with no tuft. The nest is a large pile of sticks and cactus spines constructed beneath bushes or in rocky areas, and sometimes in dead trees. The white-throated woodrat is found mainly in desert and piñon-juniper regions of the Southwest.

Desert Woodrat (Neotoma lepida). 9-14 inches long, including a 5-inch tail; the smallest of the woodrats. The nest is similar to that of the white-throated species. Found in New Mexico, Arizona, California, Nevada, Utah, and southeastern Oregon.

Dusky-Footed Woodrat (Neotoma fuscipes). 14-17 inches long, including an 8-inch tail. Found in a narrow coastal belt extending from Oregon to Baja, Mexico. These rats are exceptional climbers and generally nest in trees.

Bushy-Tailed Woodrat (Neotoma cinera). 12-17 inches long with a short, flat, very bushy tail. Found in the mountainous regions of all the western states but more commonly in Wyoming, Idaho, and Montana. The nest is usually constructed in a talus slope or a rockpile, or sometimes on a cliff face.

VOICE
Squeaks and chirps; when excited they emit a "churrr" much like that of red squirrels.

FOOD
Leaves, seeds, roots, wild nuts, and berries. Southwestern rats consume large quantities of mesquite beans and cactus fruit. Backpackers should be aware that woodrats are fond of dehydrated trail food and other snacks. Like most rodents, they store large amounts of food in their nests against hard times or cold winters.

ENEMIES
Woodrats are a valuable food source for all types of carnivores occupying the same range, especially owls. In some regions they are eaten by humans.

STATUS
Common.

THINGS YOU SHOULD KNOW
Woodrats are inquisitive nocturnal animals, usually abroad from sundown to sunrise. They are persistent thieves, spiriting away to their nest any shiny object left lying around by careless humans. In the mountains of the northern states, bushy-tailed woodrats can be camp pests, chewing pack straps, sleeping bags, and

Woodrat

dried food packages to shreds. Unhappily, they are seldom frightened away by human screeching or harassment.

It has been estimated that woodrats generally travel no more than 50 feet in any direction from their nests. They seldom need fresh water. Like kangaroo rats, they are able to absorb "metabolic water" from digesting food.

Thirteen-Lined Ground Squirrel
(Citellus tridecemlineatus)

ALIAS
Federation Ground Squirrel, Striped Gopher.

IDENTIFICATION
11 inches long, including a 5-inch tail. The basic body color is brown with light-colored underparts; the tail is wide, flat, and bushy. *The back and sides are striped with 13 narrow tan or white stripes.* The middle five stripes may be broken into spots or stars.

HABITAT
Found in southwestern Alberta (Canada), Montana, Wyoming, Colorado, Utah, Arizona, New Mexico, and Texas. Typical habitat is open prairie or mountain meadow to 10,000 feet in elevation. The den is a simple, shallow burrow, generally with only one entrance. In some, however, a tunnel may branch off to a deeper, snug nest.

Thirteen-Lined Ground Squirrel (immature)

VOICE
A shrill, churring whistle.

FOOD
About half of a thirteen-lined squirrel's diet usually consists of meat, such as mice, insects, carrion, or small birds. Occasionally they practice cannibalism when one of their species has been killed. They also consume grass, nuts, succulent plants, and garden crops.

ENEMIES
Diurnal predator birds, carnivorous mammals, and large reptiles.

STATUS
Common.

THINGS YOU SHOULD KNOW
The thirteen-lined ground squirrel is a true hibernator, sleeping underground from early September until March. However, even during warm daylight hours in the summer, this little squirrel is seen only when the sun is at full strength.

Golden-Mantled Ground Squirrel
(*Citellus lateralis*)

IDENTIFICATION
12 inches long, including a slender 4-inch tail; a small buffy ground squirrel resembling an oversized chipmunk. The underparts are light-colored, and a reddish-brown mantle covers the head and shoulders. *A wide white stripe bordered with black extends from shoulder to tail on either side of the body.* The face is plain and unstriped.

HABITAT
Found in all western states and Canada. Typical habitat is a rock-strewn slope, hillside, or mountain meadow. The den is a shallow, primitive burrow usually no more than 2 feet long with the entrance often situated between large boulders to prevent widening by predators.

VOICE
Whistles, chirps, and rapid tongue clicking ("ticking"), combined with nervous flicks of the tail.

Golden-Mantled Ground Squirrel

FOOD
Insects, nuts, seeds, berries, and garbage-can leftovers. Human handouts have little or no effect on their digestive systems.

ENEMIES
The primary enemies are weasels, which are able to pursue them into their burrows.

STATUS
Common.

THINGS YOU SHOULD KNOW
Golden-mantled ground squirrels are practiced beggars and scavengers, and many starve to death each year because they slip into National Park Service garbage cans and are unable to climb out. They are tough little animals, however, and death does not come easy. I once discovered one half-drowned after being trapped in an open garbage can during a heavy rainstorm. Using a section of rubber surgical tubing, one end of which I forced into the animal's mouth, I administered artifical respiration by blowing air into his lungs. Three

or four minutes later he awakened, bit my thumb nearly to the bone, and scurried to his burrow screeching protest all the way.

Much like thirteen-lined ground squirrels, golden-mantled ground squirrels are early hibernators, retiring for the winter by early September. During hibernation their body temperature drops to 40 degrees, and their heartbeat slows to 5 beats per minute.

Rock Ground Squirrel (*Citellus variegatus*)

ALIAS
Rock Squirrel.

IDENTIFICATION
20 inches long, including a 10-inch tail; *a large, slender squirrel, usually colored gray or brown with long, white guard hairs giving a mottled appearance.* The underparts are slightly lighter in color than the back and sides; the tail is long, slender, and heavily furred.

HABITAT
Found in the southwestern states of Arizona, Nevada, Utah, Colorado, New Mexico, and Texas, and in Mexico. Typical habitat is rocky canyon country or grassy slope below 8,000 feet in elevation. The den is an elaborate tunnel system beneath boulders or thick bushes. Not gregarious, rock squirrels prefer to live alone except during their May and August mating seasons.

VOICE
A loud whistle or "whicker."

FOOD
Traditional inhabitants of desert or arid regions, rock squirrels usually live on cactus, yucca, agave fruit, and juniper berries. If available, they will also eat small rodents, birds, carrion, garden crops, and domestic fruit.

ENEMIES
Predacious, diurnal birds, especially golden eagles and red-tailed hawks, badgers, skunks, and weasels. Commonly considered pests, rock squirrels are also hunted by man for sport.

STATUS
Common.

THINGS YOU SHOULD KNOW
Of all the ground squirrels, rock squirrels are the most unapproachable, able to disappear beneath the ground at the first hint of territorial intrusion. This unfriendly attitude is probably beneficial to man, since these squirrels are often host to large numbers of plague-carrying fleas and other harmful parasites. They should never be

Rock Ground Squirrel

handled, dead or alive.

Excellent climbers, rock squirrels often clamber about 30 or 40 feet above the ground in search of birds' nests or fresh fruit. If caught in this unprotected position, they may "freeze" for up to three hours without a single twitch.

California Ground Squirrel
(Citellus beecheyi)

IDENTIFICATION
A large, grayish ground squirrel up to 20 inches long, including a heavily furred tail. *The fur is flecked or mottled with white guard hairs, giving an overall whitish appearance.* The neck and ears are dark, either brown or gray.

HABITAT
Found throughout the western portions of California, Oregon, and the Baja Peninsula. This is the most common ground squirrel observed in the Pacific coast area. Typical habitat is open meadow or field with soft dirt for easy digging; the den is an intricate burrow. Extremely gregarious, California ground squirrels usually live in large, scurrying colonies.

VOICE
Chirps, barks, and growls.

FOOD
Along the central California coast, the diet consists of ice plant, wild strawberries, and

California Ground Squirrel

other varieties of wild fruit plants. In less abundant areas, they eat seeds, green succulent plants, and grasses.

ENEMIES
Natural predators are mainly carnivorous birds and foxes. California ground squirrel colonies are often located in protected parks and sanctuaries, beyond the reach of man.

STATUS
Common.

THINGS YOU SHOULD KNOW
The traditional range of the California ground squirrel has an exceptionally mild climate, and the animals seldom hibernate during the colder months. They are active in the daytime and generally are extremely tame.

Columbian Ground Squirrel
(Citellus columbianus)

IDENTIFICATION

A stocky, medium-sized squirrel up to 17 inches long, including a heavily furred 5-inch tail. The basic body color is brown or gray with *a reddish throat, ears, face, underparts, and tail.*

HABITAT

Found in the mountainous regions of Montana, Idaho, Oregon, and Washington at altitudes below 8,000 feet; well known to visitors of Glacier National Park and other similar mountain environments in their range. They are also commonly observed in southern Canada and occasionally as far south as New Mexico. The den is a simple burrow with at least two entrances in an open, grassy meadow. Highly gregarious, they live in colonies with populations often numbering in the hundreds depending on available food.

Columbian Ground Squirrel

VOICE
A loud, sharp, whistling "chirrrrrup."

FOOD
Succulent mountain plants, wildflowers, nuts, and roots.

ENEMIES
Predacious birds and mountain-dwelling carnivores like the weasel kill many, but colonies are usually well protected by an excellent system of sentries which whistle alarm at an intruder's approach. Wandering grizzlies are a dangerous but not serious foe.

STATUS
Common.

THINGS YOU SHOULD KNOW
Primarily a northern animal living in harsh, mountainous terrain, the Columbian ground squirrel generally retires to its burrow in late August or early September to sleep until the spring thaw. When active, however, they are friendly creatures, never so humble as to beg but residing in the vicinity of humans with little fear.

Red Squirrel
(Tamiasciurus hudsonicus)

ALIAS
Pine Squirrel, Chickaree.

IDENTIFICATION
The smallest and most nervous of tree squirrels, barely a foot in length and generally weighing less than a pound. The basic body color is reddish-gray with light underparts and nose. An easily identifiable characteristic is the red squirrel's pose—perched on a limb with its heavily furred tail curled pluckily over its back.

HABITAT
Pine, fir, and spruce forests, usually at altitudes of 6,000-10,000 feet in most western mountain ranges. Much of a red squirrel's life is spent aloft, leaping from limb to limb or poised on a wobbly twig, ready to give alarm at any intrusion. The nest is usually constructed of twigs and leaves, high in a pine or fir tree. An individual squirrel's territory seldom encompasses more than an acre or two.

VOICE
Intruders have little chance of moving unobserved or unannounced through a forest when red squirrels are present. They are alarm givers, Paul Reveres of the mountains, noisy bundles of quivering fur set off as easily as a musty blasting cap. Their most common cry is an unmistakable throaty "cheeeeeeer," combined with fits of coughing.

FOOD
A sure sign of red squirrel habitat is the midden—a large pile of pine cones, seeds, buds, and other edible items, usually located near the center of a squirrel's territory. The heap may be 15 feet in diameter and 3 feet high, and generally surrounds a large tree or stump. Occasionally these little tree squirrels consume insects, especially wood-boring beetles. They sometimes kill and eat young birds, too, but this is thought to be primarily a matter of territorial protection.

ENEMIES
Bobcats, weasels, feral housecats, hawks, and "early-bird" owls are common predators, but forest fires and lean seed years probably take a greater toll than everything else combined.

STATUS
Common.

THINGS YOU SHOULD KNOW
Red squirrels are methodical in their daily habits—a characteristic that is often fatal when predators are nearby. For example, shuttling food from forest to midden, they often use the same pathway on the ground, halting at preselected points for a quick look around. Consequently they are easy pickings for animals like bobcats, who prefer ambush tactics to the chase. They are capable of freezing into immobility for hours, however, remaining undetected while even the sharpest-eyed predators pass by within a few feet.

Red Squirrel

Tassel-Eared Squirrels

IDENTIFICATION
Sleek, gray-bodied tree squirrels with crisp white undersides and a distinctive, reddish-brown saddle down the shoulders. The tail is usually carried over the back. *Long, tufted ears thrust straight up from the head; the gait is a series of rapid, loping bounds on the ground.* The two species can be distinguished by tail color.

Abert's Tassel-Eared Squirrel (Sciurus aberti). *The tail is a large, bushy plume, gray on top, and white underneath.*

Kaibab Tassel-Eared Squirrel (Sciurus kaibabensis). Identical to Abert's squirrel except for *a pure white tail.*

HABITAT
Inhabitants of oak and pine forests above 6,000 feet, Abert's squirrels are found in Utah, Arizona, New Mexico, and Colorado. The Kaibab variety inhabits only the Kaibab Plateau in Grand Canyon National Park.

VOICE
A hearty "chu-chu-chu-chu," heard easily a mile away. They also gurgle, chatter, and "chur" when excited.

FOOD
Bark and tender shoots of the Ponderosa pine, acorns, seeds, birds' eggs, and mushrooms.

ENEMIES
Hawks are a natural predator, but perhaps the greatest threats are forest fires and lean years when food is scarce.

STATUS
Kaibab squirrels are extremely rare and are protected by Arizona state law. Abert's squirrels are a common sight to mountain visitors.

THINGS YOU SHOULD KNOW
Although designated as arboreal squirrels, tassel-ears spend much time on the ground in search of food or mischief. Seldom motionless and extremely swift, their ground gait can easily outdistance that of a human being.

Tassel-Eared Squirrels

Pika
(Ochotona princeps)

ALIAS
Coney, Cony, Rock Rabbit, Whistling Rabbit.

IDENTIFICATION
Resembles a guinea pig in size and appearance; 7-8 inches long *with no visible tail.* The basic body color is tan, cinnamon, or gray; the body is chunky, rounded, and well furred; the ears are short and dark.

HABITAT
Found from sea level to 17,000 feet in the Rocky Mountain states, Canada, California, and Alaska. Their range is the highest of any North American mammal. *Typical habitat is rockslide or rocky meadow well above timberline.* Pikas seldom venture more than 100 feet from their burrows.

VOICE
A high-pitched "Kaaaaak," voiced at intervals of four or five seconds.

FOOD
Pikas have the unique habit of gathering huge quantities of food—shrubs, berries, seeds, flowers, and especially grass and plant stems—and piling them on flat rocks next to their burrows to dry before being stored for the winter. These so-called haystacks are give-aways to pika habitat. Food is generally carried in small bundles from field to burrow in the mouth.

ENEMIES
Only two animals—martens and weasels—are capable of withstanding the rugged alpine habitat of the pika for any length of time. Both are able to pursue the pika into his network of burrows. However, pikas are gregarious, living in colonies that may number twenty or thirty. The weasel who does not capture his victim on the first try may find himself overcome by exhaustion after chasing twenty criss-crossing, fur-covered bundles of energy through what may be thousands of feet of complex tunnels. This "help your neighbor escape" routine

Pika

has been witnessed by many naturalists and seldom fails to discourage predators.

STATUS
Common.

THINGS YOU SHOULD KNOW
Pikas are susceptible to extreme heat and cold but active during the daytime in both summer and winter. They spend much of their lives in a network of passages between boulders, scurrying hither and yon even under heavy snow. Their three-ply fur is thick and heavy, well adapted for cold weather. Even their feet and ears are heavily furred for protection against frostbite. They do not hibernate.

Cottontails

ALIAS
Bunny, Puff-Tail.

IDENTIFICATION
All eight species of cottontail rabbit found in the United States are similar in appearance, and distinguishing among them in the field is difficult *except by location in accordance with name*. All are brownish-gray or tan with light-colored underparts and short ears. The tail is short, gray on top and generally white on the bottom; the hind legs are short and powerful. When frightened, cottontails tend to *hop* in erratic, zig-zag patterns, reaching speeds of 30 miles an hour over short distances. They can be distinguished from jack-rabbits by the latter's long, leaping gait.

The four species of cottontail discussed here are those observed most commonly in the western states.

Mountain Cottontail (*Sylvilagus nuttallii*).
14-17 inches long; the ears are 2½-3 inches. Found in the mountainous regions of all the western states.

Brush Rabbit (*Sylvilagus bachmani*).
12-15 inches long; the ears are 2-3 inches. Found in western Oregon, California, and the Baja Peninsula at altitudes below 5,000 feet.

Desert Cottontail (*Sylvilagus audubonii*).
Typical habitat is brushy desert or lowland in all western states except Oregon, Washington, and Idaho.

Pigmy Rabbit (*Sylvilagus idahoensis*).
10 inches long; the only western cottontail easily identified by its size. Found in eastern Oregon, northern Nevada, northern Utah, and southern Idaho.

HABITAT
Cottontails are "form" animals, resting in temporary hollows in deep grass, brush piles, or windfalls when they are not feeding. However, the brush and desert varieties occasionally inhabit underground dens for short periods of time. The nest is generally a slight depression on the ground, lined with breast fur and grass.

VOICE
When agitated, a soft, deep, growling purr, possibly accompanied by stamping of the feet. When in pain, a loud, human-like squeal.

FOOD
Primarily vegetarians, cottontails may consume carrion and their own manure (the latter probably for medicinal purposes). In areas populated by humans they may devastate alfalfa fields and garden crops.

ENEMIES
Natural predators are many: every meat-eating mammal, bird, and reptile found sharing the same range. Man is probably their greatest enemy, killing millions each year by gun and automobile. Cottontails have only a 1-in-20 chance of surviving their first year of life.

STATUS
Common.

THINGS YOU SHOULD KNOW
Besides carrying tularemia (rabbit fever), cottontails host large numbers of parasites, many of which are infectious to man. They also transport ticks, plague-carrying fleas, warble-fly larvae, tapeworms, round-worms, and flukes. Only in winter are they safe to handle or eat.

Rabbits do not hibernate and are active in both daylight and darkness. According to some naturalists, however, they "hole up" when the temperature drops below 12 degrees.

An unusual rabbit courtship is commonly observed in cottontail country. While one rabbit remains absolutely motionless, another (of the opposite sex) moves in slow circles around him, purring, growling, and stamping her feet. Suddenly the first leaps two or three feet straight into the air. The prospective mate immediately darts underneath and freezes—and the roles are reversed. The courtship ritual may last for several hours.

Cottontail (female)

Jackrabbits

ALIAS
Jack, Jackass Rabbit.

IDENTIFICATION
The two common American jackrabbits resemble each other closely. They have long, powerful hind legs that give their stride a galloping appearance; usually they leap over obstacles rather than run around them. They run with ears flat and short tail tucked tightly between their haunches. Jackrabbits are active both day and night.

Black-Tailed Jackrabbit
(Lepus californicus). 1½-2 feet long, weighing about 7 pounds. Black-tails are dull gray with white sides and underparts; *the top of the tail and ear tips are black;* the ears are 7-8 inches long. Found in all the western states, Canada, Mexico, and the Baja Peninsula, but rarely seen in Wyoming and Montana. Typical habitat is desert, open plain, or rugged foothills.

White-Tailed Jackrabbit
(Lepus towsendii). Slightly larger than black-tails, weighing up to 10 pounds. The ear tips are black *but the tail is totally white;* the ears are 6-7 inches long. Found in all western states but very seldom observed in California, Arizona, New Mexico, and Texas.

HABITAT
Jackrabbits rest or sleep in "forms" beneath clumps of grass, bushes, or cactus. They do not inhabit holes or burrows. Their territories are seldom more than two or three miles across.

VOICE
During the spring and summer mating seasons, males growl. When in pain, both sexes squeal, a sound that hunters often record and use to lure jackrabbit predators.

FOOD
Some 90 percent of a jackrabbit's diet consists of grass, though they will eat almost any vegetable matter including cactus.

ENEMIES

One of the swiftest animals in the United States, these long-legged plains dwellers are capable of 40-mile-per-hour spurts, but they are often outfoxed by coyotes and feral dogs, who either chase them down in relays or wait in ambush. Man controls jackrabbit populations by gun and automobile, then eradicates predators, allowing the number of jackrabbits to climb once again.

STATUS

Common, though only 2 in every 500 reach adulthood.

THINGS YOU SHOULD KNOW

Jackrabbits are not really rabbits but hares, born fully furred with their eyes open, ready to fend for themselves almost immediately. True rabbits (cottontails) are born blind, hairless, and helpless, dependent on their parents for food, shelter, and protection.

The stride of an adult jackrabbit in a hurry may be 20 feet long and 5 feet off the ground. They have a unique habit called "spy-hopping"—leaping higher than normal every five or six strides in order to pinpoint their pursuer. When in extreme danger, jacks erect their rump hair into "flags" by contracting layers of subcutaneous muscles. The signal probably warns other jacks in the vicinity. Another protective characteristic is the position of a jackrabbit's eyes, which are located on the sides of the head to allow vision simultaneously in front, to the side, and behind.

Mating season in jackrabbit country finds adults leaping and bounding around each other in ritual courtship dances. Competing males sometimes spar and box for female favors.

Black-Tailed Jack Rabbit

Varying Hare
(Lepus americanus)

ALIAS
Snowshoe Hare, Gray Hare.

IDENTIFICATION
16-20 inches long; the body structure resembles that of a large, lean cottontail except for the varying hare's large, heavily furred feet, which act as snowshoes in deep snow cover. The ears are 3-4 inches long. The basic summer body coloration is silky grayish brown, with white hindfeet; the belly and underside of the tail are white. During early autumn the fur begins to fade, and by winter the animal is pure white except for black or dusky ear tips. However, in the Cascade Range of Washington and Oregon and the Sierra Nevada of California, the varying hare remains grayish brown throughout the year.

HABITAT
Found in the mountainous regions of all western states except Nevada, Arizona, and southern New Mexico. Found also in Alaska and Canada. Typical habitat is a brushy mountain slope, thicket, or swamp. Varying hares do not particularly like the forest and usually stay clear of heavy timber. Most of the day is spent resting in "forms" or hollow logs. Feeding takes place during the late evenings or at night.

VOICE
A squeal when in pain.

FOOD
Grass, roots, succulent plants, leaves, and wildflowers. When winter food supplies are low, the diet consists mainly of fir bark and needles. If nothing else is available, they often girdle aspen trees by chewing away bark around the base.

ENEMIES
Varying hares are subject to cyclic and dramatic population declines thought to result from a degeneration of liver tissue called "shock disease." They are also the primary protein source for mountain-dwelling carnivores like weasels, owls,

Varying Hare (snowshoe)

and especially the Canada lynx. The hare's only defense is its camouflage and speed; adults can leap eight or ten feet per bound and make four bounds per second.

STATUS
Common in northern states; unusual in the south.

THINGS YOU SHOULD KNOW
The unusual color change from silky brown to pure white in the fall and back in the spring takes about ten weeks from start to finish, normally beginning on the ears and feet and progressing toward the tail. Since the new color is evident before actual shedding of the old color begins, biologists believe there are two sets of hair roots—one active in the fall, and the other in the spring.

In some regions varying hares are trapped extensively. Their fur is sold under the label of Baltic Fox.

Prairie Dogs

ALIAS
Farmers and ranchers in prairie dog country have given these little creatures many aliases, most of which are unprintable.

IDENTIFICATION
The two most common western species are easily distinguished.

Black-Tailed Prairie Dog (Cynomys ludovicianus). 18
inches high; the basic body color is light brown or cream; *the rear third of the short tail is totally black.* In prime form black-tails are fat, robust, and heavily furred. They are found throughout the United States, Canada, and Mexico but are rare west of Colorado or east of the Great Plains. Typical habitat is lowland prairie or desert *below 5,000 feet.* Black-tails are gregarious, and prairie dog towns 250 miles long and 50 miles wide containing an estimated 100 million inhabitants were once common. The towns are a series of mounds, each having a cluster of burrow entrances. *Each entrance is usually completely encircled by a dirt dike to protect the burrow from flooding.*

White-Tailed Prairie Dog (Cynomys gunnisoni). 14
inches high; the basic body color is gray or dark brown; *the rear third of the short tail is white or gray.* Even in good conditions white-tails are normally slender. They are found throughout the western United States, Canada, and Mexico, typically in mountain meadows or high plateaus. Not as gregarious as their larger cousins, white-tails generally live in small towns containing only a few animals or burrows. *The protective dikes around the burrow entrances are on one side only, usually at the back.*

VOICE
Normal conversation consists of chirps, barks, buzzes, and whistles. Prairie dogs also have a unique habit of standing upright near the edge of their burrow, suddenly throwing back their head and front paws,
giving a hair-curling screech, then falling forward into their burrow. This dramatic behavior is thought to be a danger signal, and some biologists even think it may be a reenactment of death meant to frighten nearby dogs into their burrows.

FOOD
Plains grasses, especially grama, flowers, and shrubs. Occasional meat eaters, prairie dogs consume small rodents, carrion, birds' eggs, and some insects.

ENEMIES
Coyotes, badgers, skunks, owls, birds of prey, and weasels sometimes sneak past an effective system of sentries to kill an old or feeble dog. The primary enemies, however, are large rattlesnakes who often enter the burrow, lying in ambush in or near the nest.

STATUS
Massive organized campaigns by ranchers using poison gas and traps have nearly put prairie dogs on the Endangered Species list. Two spe-

Black-Tailed Prairie Dog (male)

cies, in fact, the Arizona and Mexican prairie dogs, are now protected by federal law.

The demise of this little plains dog has had devastating effects on other wildlife communities. At one time prairie dogs were the almost exclusive diet of a small, voracious member of the weasel family known as the black-footed ferret. Today, because its food source is so depleted, the ferret is endangered and probably the rarest mammal in the United States. Coyotes, too, consumed large numbers of prairie dogs, especially in the endless grassy plains of the Midwest where little else was available. When the dog disappeared, the coyotes resorted to attacking livestock.

THINGS YOU SHOULD KNOW
Prairie dog towns are generally constructed in open, brushless areas providing their inhabitants with an uninterrupted view of their surroundings. If such areas are not available, an army of gleaners immediately clears all vegetation from

White-Tailed Prairie Dog

the burrow vicinity up to a distance of 60 yards. The burrows themselves are as carefully constructed as expensive homes. A few inches below the diked entrance, prairie dogs can perch in a small cavity called a listening post to outwait unwanted visitors. Below that, the burrow drops almost vertically for 15 feet, and at the bottom it branches into several horizontal tunnels—one is used as a toilet, another contains a grass-lined nest, and a third is for food storage. Most burrows have at least one rear entrance dug with care to a point just below the surface. The earthen lid protects the hole from rain, but a retreating dog can dig through to freedom in a matter of seconds.

The main reason for the widespread destruction of prairie dogs by ranchers was their competition for range grass with domestic livestock, a fact that is unfortunate but true. In addition, prairie dog burrows create a hazard for wandering horses and cattle, and the dogs themselves often host plague-carrying fleas.

MEDIUM-SIZED MAMMALS

Opossum
(Didelphis marsupialis)

ALIAS
Possum.

IDENTIFICATION
A slow-moving, nocturnal mammal, 2-3 feet long, including an almost naked, rat-like, 1-foot tail; the fur is grayish-white and very long; the feet and legs are black; the toes are white; the tail is black at the base; the ears are naked flaps of skin, usually black.

HABITAT
Transplanted in California, Oregon, and Washington; native in eastern Colorado, New Mexico, and Texas. Generally a lowland dweller, the opossum's typical habitat is temperate foothill or farmland, usually near water. The den may be beneath any suitable structure offering shelter, especially piles of brush or debris. An individual opossum's territory is seldom more than a few acres.

FOOD
Omnivorous; insects, plants, grain, garbage, mushrooms,

Opossum (female with young)

garden crops, small, slow-moving rodents, and carrion.

ENEMIES
Neither courageous nor intelligent, opossums are preyed upon by every carnivore found in their home range including domestic dogs. Their senses, especially vision, are so poorly developed that predators can easily sneak up on them undetected, but since man has removed many of their natural predators and opossums are both promiscuous and prolific breeders, their range and numbers are increasing slowly but steadily.

STATUS
Rare.

THINGS YOU SHOULD KNOW
The opossum is America's only native marsupial, a survivor of an ancient animal population that is noticeably different from modern mammals. For example, female marsupials have a stomach pouch covering the teats—a structure replaced by the placenta in less primitive creatures. After a gestation

period of just 12 days, baby opossums less than half an inch long clamber from the birth canal to the mother's pouch, there attaching themselves to one of 13 nipples, where they remain immobile for more than two months while development continues. Another marsupial trait is a set of 50 poorly developed teeth barely adequate for eating. The female also has a double womb, and the male a forked (bifurcate) penis.

An opossum's long, naked tail is prehensile and is often used as a fifth limb. Individuals have been observed carrying nesting material in its slender tip. Their only workable defense against predation is an unusual habit called "playing possum." When threatened, the animal's system reacts automatically, throwing the brain and nervous system into a catatonic state which dramatically lowers heartbeat and respiration. For all practical purposes, the animal is dead, and may consequently escape real death.

Marmots

ALIAS
Western Woodchuck, Rock-chuck, Whistler, Rock Pig, Ground Hog.

IDENTIFICATION
Marmots are very large, squirrel-like mountain dwellers, 36-40 inches long, including a heavily furred tail. The two western species described below can best be distinguished by body color.

Yellow-Bellied Marmot (*Marmota flaviventris*). *The basic body color is frosted brown or yellow with light-colored underparts.* Found in every western state except Texas. Backpackers hiking at alpine levels often hear the yellow-bellied marmot's call—a single, high-pitched "chirrruuuup!"

Hoary Marmot (*Marmota caligata*). Similar to the yellow-bellied marmot except for a *silver-gray or black and white coloration*, especially on the forelimbs. The tail is not as

Yellow-Bellied Marmot (male)

heavily furred as the yellow-bellied marmot. Found in Montana, Idaho, Washington, Canada, and Alaska. The hoary marmot's voice is a *loud whistle*, an almost human sound that can be heard for more than a mile.

HABITAT
Marmots are found at elevations of 4,000-12,000 feet. Their dens may be in mountain meadows but are more commonly located in talus slopes and rockslides. As protection against predation, their burrows are often at least 40 feet long with entrances shored up with boulders.

FOOD
Vegetarian; grass, roots, seeds, wild berries, succulent plants.

ENEMIES
Alert, agile, and sure-footed, marmots are capable of traveling at 10 miles an hour over terrain a mountain goat would balk at. Consequently, few predators are fast enough to catch them. Coyotes, foxes, wolves, bobcats, and occasionally mountain lions try, often deserting the effort with empty stomachs and sore feet. Bears, especially grizzlies, are the most persistent foe, sometimes able to dig the marmot from its burrow.

STATUS
Common. The common woodchuck, an eastern variety of marmot, is considered a pest and hunted heavily. Western species, however, because of their rugged habitat, are generally left to themselves.

THINGS YOU SHOULD KNOW
Marmots are true hibernating animals, placing themselves into a deep torpor for about 9 months of the year. Like all rodents, they have continually growing front incisors, usually kept at a practical length by constant gnawing. In some cases, however, erratic teeth may spiral crookedly from the gum line and cause death either by starvation or by growing into the eye and piercing the brain.

Hoary Marmot

Porcupine
(Erethizon dorsatum)

ALIAS
Porky, Quill Pig, Hedgehog.

IDENTIFICATION
Large, chunky animals, 2½-3 feet long, weighing up to 25 pounds. The basic body color varies from grizzled yellow to a dull green (northern states). The outer skin is spined from the cheeks to the blunt tail with hollow, multicolored quills.

HABITAT
South American natives relatively new to the United States, porcupines have migrated to every western state, Canada, and Alaska. Their typical habitat is forest, since they depend on trees for both food and shelter. They are commonly observed above timberline, however, or in the lowland deserts of the Southwest. Their dens may be in shallow caves, beneath large rocks, or in hollow trees. During the winter porcupines usually prefer sunny mountain slopes or ridges where the snow melts quickly. They do not hibernate and are active both day and night.

VOICE
Grunts, squeals, moans, whines, and meows. When excited, they click and grind their teeth.

FOOD
Natural food is pine and willow bark, mistletoe, conifer needles, wild berries, nuts, and wildflowers. Porcupines have a constant craving for salt and will consume anything that contains even the slightest trace of it. In several instances they have attempted to eat shoes—while humans were still wearing them! In many regions park rangers and game officials find it necessary to transport campground porcupines to distant locations because their gnawing at salty or soapy wood in outdoor bathrooms is so destructive.

ENEMIES
Motorists and forest fires kill hundreds of thousands of these slow, deliberate creatures each

Porcupine (female)

year, but natural predators are few. Carnivores unfamiliar with a porcupine's defense system may find their muzzles filled with needle-sharp quills, which in rare cases penetrate the eyes and cause immediate death. More likely, however, the quills result in slow starvation for the unfortunate victim. More patient animals like mountain lions have learned to flip the porcupine onto its back by slipping a paw beneath the unspined stomach.

STATUS
Common.

THINGS YOU SHOULD KNOW
A porcupine has about 30,000 quills, ranging in length from ¼ inch on the face to over 4 inches on the back and tail. In addition, the quills themselves are covered with thousands of microscopic "fish-scale" barbs. The porcupine cannot throw them, but it can stand them on end at will by contracting a layer of subcutaneous muscles. When in danger, porcupines turn their hindquarters toward the enemy and strike with the tail.

Because of an ability to flatten her quills along her body, a female can copulate without lacerating her mate. Obviously, however, there is no such thing as rape in the porcupine world. The young are born surrounded by a membranous sac which protects the mother's uterus and birth canal from puncture.

Adult porcupines spend half their lives in trees, often sleeping perched on a limb when no other shelter is available. Their eyesight and other senses are poorly developed, and they are one of the few wild animals man can dispatch with only a stick if need be. The meat is tough but edible.

Coatimundi
(*Nasua narica*)

ALIAS
Coati, Cholla.

IDENTIFICATION
A long-faced, dog-like animal, 3-4 feet in length, including a very *long, banded tail usually carried straight up or at a 45-degree angle*. The basic body color is grizzled yellow or reddish-brown with slightly lighter underparts. The snout is extremely long and pointed, and normally covered with tough gristle as a result of constant rooting for food. The face is banded with black or brown; the gait is a flat-footed gallop.

Coatimundi (tail)

HABITAT
Found in extreme southern Texas, New Mexico, and Arizona as well as Mexico. Typical habitat is rocky canyon or open desert. In Mexico coatis are jungle dwellers. The females are gregarious and may run in large troops, but the males usually prefer bachelorhood except during an April mating season. They are active both day and night.

VOICE
A pack of coatis represents the nearest thing to a treeful of howling monkeys the desert ecosystem has to offer. Their most common utterances are screeches, hisses, gabbles, and howls.

FOOD
Omnivorous; since coati range is primarily desert, the diet consists of cactus fruits, wild nuts, small rodents, birds' eggs, frogs, and lizards.

ENEMIES
Natural predators are few. In Mexico coatis are probably killed by the larger predatory

Coatimundi

cats. In the United States they are molested only by man, especially in his automobile.

STATUS
Uncommon.

THINGS YOU SHOULD KNOW
Coatis are clowns, always squabbling or playing, seemingly unconcerned with their surroundings. They are among the best climbers in North America, able to move almost as well aloft as on the ground. They quite often hang from a limb by their hind feet while feeding or playing. The long, limber tail is not prehensile but can be used as a balancing aid.

One coati tactic is quite unique to the species. If surprised while aloft, a coati may just let go and fall to the ground, no matter what position he might have been in. While the intruder looks for the flattened remains, the coati scrambles away to safety.

Raccoon
(Procyon lotor)

ALIAS
Coon, Masked Bandit, Midnight Marauder.

IDENTIFICATION
A roly-poly, furry mammal, 3-3½ feet long including the tail, 12 inches high at the shoulder, and weighing 25-40 pounds. One word describes the raccoon—cute. He is a bundle of grayish-brown fur with glittering eyes, long whiskers, and a heavily furred, dramatically ringed tail. A narrow black mask across a hatchet-like face and two white patches above the eyes make him look like the Lone Ranger.

Raccoon (tail)

HABITAT
Raccoons are found in all the western states, southern Canada, Mexico, and South America, but *not* in a narrow belt running southward from northern Idaho to southern California or above 6,000 feet in elevation. Their typical habitat varies from region to region. It may be a swampy or watery area, a garbage dump, a city park, a desert, or a forest. The den may be a cave or burrow, but most commonly it is located in a hollow tree.

VOICE
The raccoon's vocal chords are advanced enough to allow a large variety of sounds ranging from growls to whines, screeches, grunts, laughs, giggles, hoots, and snores.

FOOD
Omnivorous. With great gusto raccoons devour whatever the environment provides. Meat, rotted or otherwise, insects, crayfish, nuts, berries, freeze-dried food (from camper's packs), eggs, snakes—whatever they can catch or find they will consume. Some are particularly fond of bird meat, especially the kind that comes from a henhouse. Others enjoy dirty diapers, candy bar wrappers, eggshells, and the entire range of smelly human waste products stored in trash cans. Their appetites are enormous, their preferences few.

ENEMIES
Many would-be predators have wobbled away on three legs after an encounter with a raccoon's razor-sharp teeth and irascible temper. Humans, dog packs, traps, and automobiles are his greatest enemies, since few others can handle an adult raccoon with his dander up.

STATUS
Common. About 1.5 million raccoons are killed each year for their fur and sold as Alaska Bear or Alaska Sable. Their skins bring about $30 each. However, female raccoons are promiscuous and their litters are large, usually four to seven pups a year. The young are up and about in 20 days, hunting in 10 weeks, and on their own in a year. Happily, raccoon populations are reasonably stable.

THINGS YOU SHOULD KNOW
The rumor that coons always wash their food before eating is false. They will generally eat anything, anytime, anywhere, dirty or not. (I've seen a raccoon pick up sections of rotted beef gristle that were probably stale in the time of Hannibal, pop them in his mouth, and swallow with the greatest delight, never once looking around for a washbasin.)

Raccoons are nocturnal animals, preferring to sleep away the daylight hours in some cozy den. In cold country they may sleep for a good portion of the winter. Young raccoons make excellent pets but should be handled with care especially during feeding time and released to the wild before they are a year old. They revert back to nature quickly and seldom suffer from culture shock.

Raccoon

Long-Tailed Weasel
(Mustela frenata)

ALIAS
American Ermine.

IDENTIFICATION
A short-legged, snake-like mammal, 15-20 inches long, including a *7-inch, black-tipped tail.* The summer coloration is brown with chin and underparts yellowish-white. During the winter the color is pure white except for the black-tipped tail. The gait is a bounding lope. Long-tailed weasels with a black-masked face (bridled weasels) live in some parts of the Southwest.

Two similar species, the least weasel and the short-tailed weasel, also exist in the United States but are not commonly observed. The least weasel (Mustela rixosa) is 7-9 inches long with a light-colored 1½-inch tail. The short-tailed variety (Mustela erminea) is 9-14 inches long with a 3-inch tail. Both species turn white in winter.

HABITAT
Found in Alaska, Canada, and all western states except extreme southern California and the western half of Arizona, in all types of terrain. The den may be in a burrow or hollow log, beneath a rockpile, or even in the den of an animal recently devoured.

VOICE
Barks, growls, hisses, snarls, and screeches. All three species also emit a powerful musk used both as a defensive weapon and as a means of communicating with other weasels.

FOOD
Voracious eaters, weasels kill and consume any animal—bird, mammal, or reptile—small enough to handle. The mainstay of their diet, however, is field mice.

ENEMIES
A weasel's natural predators are owls and other birds of prey. Man commonly traps weasels for their fur. However, a weasel's worst enemy is

another member of his own species. Weasel populations have a built-in control, since one weasel cannot abide living near another except during the July mating season. When the population becomes too high, fierce and deadly territorial battles take place in which one animal, normally the weaker female, is always killed.

STATUS

Common, but rarely seen because of their extremely wary nature.

THINGS YOU SHOULD KNOW

In *Life Histories of Northern Animals*, the naturalist Ernest Thompson Seton states: "No creature that lives is more thoroughly possessed of the lust for blood than the slim-bodied weasel. They hunt tirelessly, following their prey by scent, and kill for the mere joy of killing, often leaving their victims uneaten and hurrying on for more." These busy creatures are active both day and night.

The weasel's black-tipped tail seems to serve him well as a protective distraction. Attacking predator birds usually strike at the more visible black tip, missing the body entirely.

Long-Tailed Weasel

Skunks

ALIAS
Polecat.

IDENTIFICATION
Two principal western species are described below.

Striped Skunk (*Mephitis mephitis*). 20-30 inches long, including the wide, bushy tail; the body color is glossy black striped with white. *The face is bisected by a narrow white stripe* which extends to the neck, divides into two wide bands, and runs the length of the body. Found in all western states, Canada, and Mexico in all types of terrain. A skunk's territory may consist of 30 or 40 acres. Striped skunks are active both day and night.

Spotted Skunk (*Spilogale putorius*). 15-25 inches long, including the tail. *The body color is black and white, patched or striped;* the head is splotchy; *the tip of the long black tail is generally white.* Found in all western states except Montana and Wyoming.

Striped Skunk

Their dens are usually caves or burrows. Spotted skunks are primarily nocturnal.

VOICE
A low growl.

FOOD
Omnivorous. Skunks often travel 5 to 10 random miles within their territory each night, searching for field mice or other small rodents, birds, eggs, garbage, and insects. They are adept at raiding garbage cans, whether in a mountain campground or in downtown Denver.

ENEMIES
Neither automobiles nor great horned owls are deterred by a skunk's stinky displays, and both kill large numbers each year. Skunk fur was once dyed for coats and collars, but a new law requiring all fur garments to be labeled with the fur's true name halted most human predation.

STATUS
Common.

THINGS YOU SHOULD KNOW
The chemical agent skunks spray at their enemies is a powerful sulfur compound called n-bulylmercaptan. It is ejected in a fan-like pattern from two small openings near the animal's rectum. The glands containing the chemical hold enough for four or five full-powered shots, but skunks seldom spray without warning or cause. At the approach of an intruder they may stamp their forepaws and growl if flight is impossible. If that doesn't work, they wheel and lift their bushy tail into a plume position. If the intruder still persists, the body is drawn into an inverted horseshoe position and the chemical ejected. At 40 feet they seldom miss.
Never throw rocks at a skunk and never stand downwind from some fool who is doing so. From experience I can say that n-bulylmercaptan carries 100 feet or more on a good breeze, and the only way to get rid of the smell is to get rid of your clothes, usually by burning them. Tomato juice works well to cleanse the skin.

Badger
(Taxidea taxus)

IDENTIFICATION
2-2½ feet long, weighing 20-30 pounds; a sturdy, long-haired member of the weasel family *conspicuously flattened in appearance*. The basic body color is grizzled brownish-gray with black feet and face; the nose is bisected by a distinctive white stripe; the tail and legs are short; the front feet are armed with long, heavy digging claws. A badger's personality is, to say the least, inflammable.

HABITAT
Found from sea level to 10,000 feet in all the western states, southern Canada, and Mexico. Typical badger habitat is generally treeless, with soft soil or sand available for easy digging. Badger dens may be enlarged former rodent burrows or freshly dug deep chambers up to 60 feet long. Badgers do not hibernate but sometimes sleep during cold spells.

FOOD
Carnivorous; rodents, ground squirrels, chipmunks, carrion, skunks, snakes, eggs, and ground-dwelling birds. Kills are sometimes buried for later consumption.

VOICE
A threatening growl-hiss combination; also grunts and purrs.

ENEMIES
Because of its large size, sharp teeth, and claws, and a furious reaction to territorial intruders, the American badger has few natural predators. A few are destroyed by man when their burrows become a hazard to domestic livestock. They were once commercially trapped and their fur used as bristles for shaving brushes.

STATUS
Common.

THINGS YOU SHOULD KNOW
Extraordinary courage and unpredictability makes the badger an animal to be avoided if possible. Normally badgers flee or burrow themselves into hiding when humans are near, but occasional attacks

have been reported. I was once attacked and very literally treed by a large female when I unknowingly intruded on her territory.

The burrowing ability of these large weasels is amazing. In soft soil, using their claws and teeth like a steam shovel, adults can dig themselves into the ground and out of sight in a few seconds, plugging the hole behind with dirt. Another defensive device is a powerful, musky scent much like that of a skunk, emitted when the creature is frightened. As an added precaution against predators, a set of heavy muscles around the neck and throat make it difficult to obtain a killing hold.

During the 1800's badgers gained an infamous reputation as grave robbers because they commonly dug into human burial sites. They were thought to consume human corpses, but in reality the soft cemetery earth made ideal homesites or hunting grounds.

Badger

Kit Fox
(Vulpes macrotis)
(Vulpes velox)

ALIAS
Desert Fox, Swift Fox, Big-Eared Fox.

IDENTIFICATION
America's smallest fox. Less than 3 feet long, including the tail, and weighing 3-6 pounds, the kit fox resembles a small, light-colored dog. Several species exist in the United States, but for all practical purposes they differ only in range. The basic body color is light gray or buff yellow; *the tail is full and tipped in black*; the ears are dark brown and extremely long.

HABITAT
Found at lower altitudes in all western states except Idaho and Washington. Typical habitat is generally open plain, desert, or plateau, with sandy soil for easy digging. The burrow may be 15 feet long with several entrances; it is usually perfectly round, not oblong like a coyote burrow. The animals are normally nocturnal.

Kit Fox

VOICE
Chattering, squirrel-like barks; when angry or in pain, sharp growls.

FOOD
Kangaroo rats, ground squirrels, rabbits, and insects. Kit foxes prefer to bring their prey to the den instead of devouring it in the field as most carnivores do.

ENEMIES
Blessed with neither the cunning nor the wariness of other wild dog species, these little foxes often fall prey to poisoned baits and steel traps set for coyotes. This single factor has led to a dramatic decline in kit fox populations during the last 50 years. Natural predators are coyotes and predacious birds.

STATUS
Uncommon. The San Joaquin (a California subspecies) kit fox has been placed on the Endangered Species list.

THINGS YOU SHOULD KNOW
Of all the wild dogs, the elfin kit fox is the least adaptable and most infrequently seen. Where man is present, they retreat; by now they have been driven into wastelands where humans do not reside. They do, however, have varied reactions to human contact. I once discovered a kit fox caught in a steel trap, its foreleg mangled. Since it was late afternoon, the animal had probably been captive for at least 12 hours. After 10 minutes of struggle during which I barely escaped losing a finger or three several times, I finally got him loose and stood back to watch him flee. Instead of promptly disappearing behind the nearest bush, he limped a few paces, turned, and stared, the look on his small, pointed face asking WHY? Needless to say, the trapper never found his trap.

Gray Fox
(Urocyon cinereo-argenteus)

ALIAS
Tree Fox.

IDENTIFICATION
A slender, dog-like animal, 3-4 feet long, including a bushy tail; the average weight is 8-14 pounds. The basic body color is *grizzled gray with a distinctive black streak down the top of the tail*. The ears, neck, legs, shoulders, and feet are usually reddish-brown; the muzzle is black.

HABITAT
The most common fox in western America, the gray fox is found in all western states except Washington, Idaho, Montana and Wyoming. Gray foxes are generally considered mountain animals, but they also live in low, brushy areas, deciduous forests, and swamps. Their dens may be located in hollow logs, in windfalls, and occasionally in trees. A fox's territory encompasses about 100 acres.

VOICE
A loud, harsh yap.

FOOD
Mice, rats, rabbits, eggs, game birds, frogs, and domestic fruit crops like watermelons, apples, and peaches; carrion, poultry, and newborn lambs are occasionally consumed.

ENEMIES
Natural predators are eagles, bobcats, and coyotes. Gray foxes are trapped heavily by man for their fur.

STATUS
Common.

THINGS YOU SHOULD KNOW
Unlike the red fox, a near cousin, the gray fox seldom leads intruders a merry chase, preferring instead to disappear into a thicket or hole, or up a tree. Gray foxes are excellent climbers, able to hook their paws over low branches and pull themselves up. Their top speed is only about 20 miles an hour, far slower than other American foxes. This handicap probably accounts for their hiding instinct.

Gray Fox

Red Fox
(Vulpes fulva)

ALIAS
Reynard, Colored Fox, Cross Fox.

IDENTIFICATION
3-3½ feet long, weighing 5-10 pounds. The basic body color is gold or red with light-colored underparts and black feet. The ears are large and triangular; the eyes are gold; *the tail is long, bushy, and tipped with white.* The cross fox, a color variation of the red fox, is brownish-yellow with bisecting black bands down the back and across the shoulders.

HABITAT
Found in heavily forested regions, farmlands, meadows, brushy lowlands, fence rows, and marshy areas of all western states, Canada, and Alaska. Red fox burrows may be up to 50 feet in length with 10 different entrances. Den identification can usually be made from fox hair near the main entrance as well as piles of bird wings, bones, and other animal remains. Strangely enough, though their dens are elaborate, the foxes themselves prefer to remain in the open, even during heavy snow.

VOICE
Short yelps (male) or yapping squeals (female).

FOOD
Red foxes greatly enjoy an occasional chicken dinner and are commonly observed "prowling the coop" in search of a lonesome pullet or three. They are, however, omnivorous, feeding upon small mammals, birds, fruits, wild berries, and even grass. Large males sometimes attack fawns, lambs, or muskrats.

ENEMIES
As the naturalist Victor Cahalane says so aptly in *Mammals of North America*, "All its life the red fox has a struggle to keep its glossy, golden-red fur coat on its back. Someone is always trying to snatch it. The trapper is after the fox with a bundle of clanking steel traps and stock of tricks. The angry farmer is

out with a shotgun to avenge some missing poultry. Finally there comes the dog, to which the scent of fox is both tantalizing and maddening, a perpetual challenge to speed and intelligence.''

STATUS
Common.

THINGS YOU SHOULD KNOW
Unlike the male sex of most other wild animals, papa red fox takes an important and active part in raising his pups, supplying his mate and children with food, care, and training. Normally, however, males live apart from their families, visiting much of the day or night but sleeping elsewhere.

Crossing open areas, the red fox sometimes carries his tail in a plume position, possibly to fool large predator birds into striking high at the tail instead of the body.

When prey is not immediately needed by the young, red foxes often cache it beneath leaves or grass for future consumption.

Red Fox

Coyote
(Canis latrans)

ALIAS
Prairie Wolf, Brush Wolf, Little Wolf.

IDENTIFICATION
A large but scrawny dog-like animal, 4-4½ feet long, including the tail; the average weight is 30-50 pounds. The basic body color is gray, brown, or light tan; a light-colored under-pelt gives the animal a splotchy appearance. The ears are long and pointed; the tail is heavily furred, often tipped in black or brown, and usually carried low or between the rear legs.

HABITAT
Found throughout the western United States, Canada, and Mexico from sea level to 10,000 feet in elevation and sometimes higher. Coyotes live as comfortably in suburbia as in a wilderness area, however. An individual animal's territory may vary from a few hundred acres to 100 square miles depending on available food supplies. Coyote dens are usually underground, beneath the roots of larger trees, or dug into a dirt hill or gully. In flatland regions with little cover, coyotes often den beneath highway culverts.

VOICE
Coyotes are not afraid to voice their displeasure or contentment no matter who might be listening. They howl, yip, bark, yowl, yelp, and screech. The most common utterance is a long, mournful howl at dusk or shortly before dawn; the most unusual is a series of sharp yips and yowls lasting up to a minute, usually indicating a fresh kill or territorial dispute.

FOOD
Coyotes consume whatever is handy and easy to catch, be it vegetable, meat, or garbage. They prey upon the entire range of small mammals as well as game birds, waterfowl, eggs, garden crops, reptiles, fish, domestic livestock (mainly sheep), carrion, plastic, rubber, and occasionally metal of one kind or another. Generally, location dictates the daily entree. For example, north-western coyotes survive almost exclusively on dead salmon in season, whereas more civilized animals residing within city limits live mainly on garbage. In northern Mexico, where small game is scarce, coyotes consume great quantities of carrion, usually dead cattle or horses killed by automobiles along the highway. In coastal areas they may survive totally on crabs, dead sea birds, or rotting fish.

ENEMIES
Natural predators are few; the main enemies are trappers, either private or federal, hired by the beef and wool industries. More than 150,000 are killed each year because they prey heavily on lambs and calves. Parasites and rabies take a few. sites and rabies take a few.

STATUS
Whether or not coyotes should be considered an Endangered Species depends on which expert is voicing his opinion at the time. According to U.S. Department of Agriculture reports, coyotes kill between 800,000 and 1,000,000 sheep annually. That figure should probably be quartered, since coyotes are carrion eaters and are often sighted at carcasses killed by natural causes. Even so, it is a record an endangered animal could hardly produce.

Coyote populations vary with location, of course. During 1974 coyotes in New Mexico were so numerous and food was in such demand that several attacks on human beings were reported and documented. In other regions, however, coyote populations are so low that mice and rats have reached pest levels and are destroying farmers' crops.

THINGS YOU SHOULD KNOW
Few animals are as sly, crafty, and well suited for survival as the coyote. He can eat anything, live anywhere in any type of climate, and left to his own devices, reproduce prolifically (record litters of 19 pups have been reported). He has been the subject of massive campaigns mounted by ranchers using traps, aircraft, dogs, and

a particularly devastating device called an M-44 cyanide gun (also called a coyote-getter)—a small tube of cyanide gas, baited and implanted in the ground, which explodes when disturbed, filling the air (or the animal's mouth) with gas. Yet the coyote survives and surprisingly seems to be increasing his range.

Coyotes pair for life if their mate survives. Adults can travel 45 miles an hour and run down a full-grown jackrabbit (they often hunt in pairs or packs, however, chasing game in relays). They are extremely adept at disappearing, literally able to vanish behind objects less than a foot high. They are active both day and night.

Coyote

Wolf
(Canis lupus)

IDENTIFICATION
A large, husky, dog-like animal, 4-6 feet long, including the tail; its average weight is 40-100 pounds. Coloration varies with location. Northern wolves may be gray, black, or white with lighter underparts and legs. There is often a light-colored or silver mane. Southern wolves are generally gray with a reddish-brown mane, ears, and legs. Both types have long, slender, well-proportioned legs; the tail is a large bush, often tipped in black; the head is wide and flat; the muzzle is blunt.

HABITAT
Found in Alaska, Canada, extreme southern New Mexico, and Texas. Undocumented sightings have been reported in Wyoming and Montana. A few animals still exist in Minnesota, Wisconsin, and Michigan. Typical habitat in the north is heavy timber near water; southern wolves prefer brushy grassland or desert.

Both varieties are usually pack animals, and territories may encompass 100 square miles. Wolf dens may be enlarged coyote burrows or other subterranean dwellings, usually with more than one entrance. Territories and dens are marked with urine and protected viciously.

VOICE
The most common utterance is a long, mournful howl; wolves also bark, yip, and growl. In addition to the usual dog sounds, however, wolf packs seem to have an extensive language that includes grunts, groans, yowls, and much nose-touching and tail-wagging.

FOOD
In contrast to hundreds of legends claiming that wolf packs attack and kill adult moose and caribou, most observers say wolves take just the young, aged, or sick. A good portion of the wolf's diet consists of carrion, field mice, marmots, and any other small mammals found within their range. Wolf packs often travel 20 or 30 miles a night to hunt.

ENEMIES
No natural predators. Wolves are susceptible to rabies, mange, and distemper, which in years past have decimated their numbers. Their primary enemy, however, is man. In Alaska wolves are hunted from aircraft as well as trapped heavily for their fur.

STATUS
Endangered.

THINGS YOU SHOULD KNOW
There has never been a documented report of a wolf attacking a human being in North America, unless in self defense. Unfortunately, wolves have been labeled superbeasts, capable of wiping out entire human families or carrying stray children to their dens. These utterly ridiculous stories are in a good part responsible for the wolf's decline. One Canadian newspaper offered a sizable reward to anyone who could prove he was the victim of a wolf attack. The reward was never collected.

Of all American mammals, wolves are perhaps the best parents. Besides providing loving care and training to their own offspring, mated wolves often adopt orphans, raising them as their own. Sometimes a female with no pups may act as a second mother to another female's pups. Wolf pups are never left alone. While the pack hunts, one adult is always near the den. Adult wolves will fight to the death to protect a pup, even if it is not their own.

According to scientists wolf packs are generally led by a single dominant male who makes most of the important decisions concerning hunting trips, moves, division of food, and daily behavior. Called the Alpha Male, this wolf is usually the largest and strongest of the immediate pack. He is charged with protecting the females and pups from intruders as well as leading the pack.

Wolf

Collared Peccary
(Tayassu tajacu)

ALIAS
Javelina, Wild Pig, Desert Pig, Musk Hog.

IDENTIFICATION
A distinctly pig-like animal, 2½-3 feet long and weighing 40-60 pounds. The body color is grizzled gray with a whitish collar across the shoulders. The legs are slender and short, ending in very small hooves. There is no visible tail. Both sexes develop small, tusk-like canine teeth which can be used as defensive weapons. A large musk gland near the rectum emits a powerful, distinctive odor.

HABITAT
Found in southern Texas, New Mexico's "boot heel," and southern Arizona, usually below 6,000 feet. A subspecies ranges throughout Mexico and South America. Peccaries are desert animals, inhabiting brushy or cactus-covered regions, shallow arroyos, or rocky canyons. They make their

homes in thickets, shallow caves, or heavy brush.

VOICE
Much like that of a domestic pig: grunts and squeals, and a bark when excited.

FOOD
Roots, insects, snakes, mesquite beans, and cactus. Adults often develop calloused front knees because of their habit of kneeling while they root for food.

ENEMIES
Ferocious when cornered, peccaries have few predators except mountain lions. They are hunted by man during a limited winter season and a few are killed by automobiles.

STATUS
Rare. The peccary once ranged as far east as Arkansas and as far north as Colorado, but unrestricted hunting from 1850 until 1920 dramatically decreased their population in the United States. The largest herds inhabit Big Bend National Park and Aransas National

Collared Peccary

Wildlife Refuge, both in Texas. Estimates place their number at about 50,000.

THINGS YOU SHOULD KNOW
Peccaries are not related to the so-called "wild pig" commonly found in southern states. In fact, they are not pigs at all; their closest living relative is probably the hippopotamus.

They have acquired an unwarranted reputation for viciousness against humans. In reality, they are near-sighted herd animals, mean when cornered but extremely afraid of man. Most attacks on humans result when they are surprised and scatter in every direction to escape, sometimes directly toward the intruder. Very likely they do not realize that they are chasing the very thing that frightened them into flight. Stories of peccary herds chasing, killing, and eating human beings are totally false.

Primarily nocturnal, they sometimes venture out in early morning or late evening.

Bobcat
(Lynx rufus)

ALIAS
Wildcat, Bob-Tailed Cat.

IDENTIFICATION
2½-3 feet long, weighing 25-40 pounds; may resemble a large, spotted housecat. The basic body color varies from tan to gray; the underparts are white; *the tail is bobbed; the ears are long with 1-inch black tufts at the end.* The Canada lynx, a northern visitor sometimes seen in the United States, is similar to the bobcat but has much larger feet, longer ear tufts, and *a black-tipped tail.*

HABITAT
Found below 8,000 feet in all the western states, Mexico, and extreme southern Canada. Bobcat dens may be located in rockslides, hollow trees, highway culverts, or beneath abandoned houses in suburban areas. The size of a bobcat's territory varies with food supplies, but it may be as large as 20 square miles or as small as 2.

VOICE
During the January mating season "bobcat squalling" creates a clamor unequaled by any other wild creature. Bobcats also spit, hiss, and make a threatening, raspy growl when angry.

FOOD
Carnivorous; rats, mice, rabbits, squirrels, marmots, grouse, quail, carrion, and insects. These small cats have been accused of killing large, healthy game animals like deer and elk, but the prospect of a 30-pound bobcat bringing down an angry 200-pound mule deer or 400-pound elk is unlikely unless the prey is sick or wounded. The reports probably stem from cases where bobcats have been seen feeding on carrion. They do, however, take young lambs, chickens, and domestic turkeys.

ENEMIES
Men have been killing bobcats for profit since 1730, when their pelts brought 30 shillings each. In 1976 bobcat skins were fetching a handsome $150 from furriers, an excellent incentive for commercial trappers. Natural predators are few. Roundworms and tapeworms kill a few each year, as do automobiles.

STATUS
Common, though in some areas where trapping is heavy and continuous, they are rare. Because of a retiring personality and nocturnal habits, they are seldom observed.

THINGS YOU SHOULD KNOW
The "wildcat" alias is no misnomer. When cornered or wounded, bobcats are spirited, ferocious, and fearless, no matter what size their attacker. Their senses are so well developed, however, that humans and other intruders are usually unable to approach a healthy cat without detection.

Bobcats hunt in random, zigzag patterns, circling a bush or log several times before moving on. They seldom give chase, preferring a dinner that is easy to catch. Like most members of the cat family,

bobcats use the impact of their body to pull larger prey down, killing with a bite to the spinal cord just behind the neck.

Bobcats see well in the darkness because of a special light-reflecting adaptation to the eye's retina. It is the same mechanism that causes their eyes to glitter when caught in automobile headlights.

Bobcat

3/

LARGE MAMMALS

Mountain Lion
(Felis concolor)

ALIAS
Ghost Cat, Panther, Puma, Catamount, Screamer, Painter, Cougar.

IDENTIFICATION
7-9 feet long, including the tail; weighs 150-300 pounds. The basic body color varies from tawny tan to gray; the tail is long and heavy, tipped with brown or black. Adults in prime condition often have a paunch.

HABITAT
Found from sea level to 10,000 feet in most of the western states, western Canada, Mexico, and South America. In the east mountain lions inhabit Florida, and there have been undocumented sightings in Maine, Georgia, South Carolina, and Louisiana. Typical western habitat is steep, rocky canyon country or mountainous terrain. Territories are large, but a rigid social structure does not permit individual ranges to overlap. Individual territories are marked with "scrapes"—piles of dirt and leaves sprayed with urine. Under ordinary circumstances, mountain lion dens are rocky caves.

VOICE
The harsh, high-pitched scream of an adult mountain lion is often compared to that of a woman. It is truly terrifying but very seldom heard. Lions are generally silent except when cornered. Then they growl, snarl, and spit.

FOOD
Unlike the smaller bobcats, lions prefer the chase, often combining efforts with brother, sister, or mate for better results. Their mainstay is the mule deer, an animal so swift and wary that mountain lions are their only serious natural predators. Wandering up a mountain path shortly before twilight a few years ago, I was startled to see a young mule deer doe streak by in the underbrush, running as if the devil himself were on her heels. A heartbeat behind, ears flattened, tail streaming out, yellow teeth bared, came that very devil in the form of a young lion. Both passed by in a split second without ever realizing that their life-and-death race was being observed. The doe did not go far. As I watched her zig-zag through the trees in an attempt to lose her determined pursuer, another lion, this one lying in ambush, leaped on her back and brought her screaming to the ground. With his powerful jaws, he snapped her spinal cord just behind the neck in less time that it takes to blink. For a moment the scene was frozen—the doe lying like a broken doll, the two cats standing over her motionless. Then the lions caught my scent and with a quick glance in my direction, vanished into the forest, leaving their prey where it had fallen. Normally lions feed only lightly after a kill; then they drag their victim a few yards away and camouflage it with dirt, leaves, and small twigs. Later they return to eat their fill. I left the doe where she was and returned the following day. Her carcass had been reduced to bones and hide.

STATUS
American lion populations are caught in a deadly circle of competition for food and territory with their only predator, man. Where overhunting has significantly lowered deer populations, lions have turned to livestock, and in turn they are hunted themselves. Today the lion is an Endangered Species in Florida and rare in other states. Unfortunately, instead of receiving badly needed protection, many western lions are still being killed under conditions ranging from limited hunting seasons in some states to open season in others.

THINGS YOU SHOULD KNOW
Lion attacks on humans are rare, and the animals involved are usually starving, sick, or confused. Only one death, that of a young boy in New Mexico, has ever been attributed to a healthy cat in a documented report. Most attack reports originate with hikers or hunters who are uninformed about lion behavior. Lions are curious animals, sometimes following humans for long distances. Their purpose, however, is to satisfy a curious feline nature, not hunger.

Mountain Lion (female)

Black Bear
(Ursus americanus)

ALIAS
Cinnamon Bear, Brown Bear.

IDENTIFICATION
4-5 feet long and 2-3 feet high at the shoulder, weighing 200-400 pounds; a large brawny animal varying in color from blonde through all shades of brown to black. Black bears sometimes, but not always, have white muzzles. Their smaller size and lack of a hump above the shoulder blades distinguish them from grizzlies.

HABITAT
Found in Alaska, Canada, and all western states, though their numbers are limited in Nevada, Utah, and southern California. Typical habitat is thick forest with plentiful food. Along the Oregon, Washington, and northern California coastlines, black bears reside at sea level. In other regions they may range to above 10,000 feet. Their dens are generally in holes or caves but may be beneath fallen trees, old buildings, or under windfalls; the dens of

females are usually more elaborate (lined with leaves or grass) than those of males.

VOICE

In their daily behavior, bears are silent creatures, moving with stealth and caution through their range. Excite them, however, and their behavior changes rapidly. Frightened or angry, they "snuffle," taking in a sharp breath while giving a low bark. They also growl, whine, and "woooof."

FOOD

Omnivorous. Black bears seldom pass up anything edible, be it grass, seeds, vegetables, nuts, succulent plants, fish, eggs, or meat. Ground squirrels, chipmunks, gophers, and carrion are readily consumed because of their availability. Garbage is also a favorite.

ENEMIES

Man.

STATUS

Common, though rare in some areas because of heavy hunting pressure.

THINGS YOU SHOULD KNOW

Where natural conditions exist, black bears are not dangerous, though they may attack if angered or separated from their cubs by intruding humans. Sows with cubs are especially short-tempered and should be avoided. Unfortunately, many bears become pests in regions where they are fed by humans. Such is usually the case around national park campgrounds or garbage dumps. Backpackers in bear country should remove all food and other smelly objects from temptation by stringing them up between two trees at least 15 feet from the ground. Hikers should also be aware that leaving goodies in a tent overnight is an open invitation to unwanted guests.

All bears—blacks, grizzlies, and the big brown bears of Alaska—dislike dogs. Pets on the trail may actually attract bears instead of driving them away. Climbing a tree for safety is useless: since black bears can partially retract their claws, they can climb as well or better than humans.

Black Bear

Grizzly Bear
(Ursus arctos horribilis)

ALIAS
Silvertip, Big Brown Bear.

IDENTIFICATION
Up to 8 feet long, 3-4 feet high at the shoulder, weighing 400-1,000 pounds; a very large, shaggy bear colored dark gray to amber, but often medium brown. In some cases long, multicolored guard hairs give a frosted or grizzled appearance to the fur. *The facial structure is slightly concave (shovel-faced). There is a single, meaty hump directly over the shoulders.* Grizzlies often emit an odor reminiscent of rotting garbage and skunk. The smell is not a musk but the result usually of rolling in carrion.

HABITAT
In the lower United States grizzlies are found only in Idaho, Montana, and Wyoming. They are wide-ranging in Alaska and western Canada. Undocumented reports place them in New Mexico, Colorado, Utah, and Washington, but the

Grizzly Bear

possibility is unlikely. A subspecies, the Mexican grizzly (*Ursus arctos nelsonii*), is said to inhabit the Sierra Madre 50 miles north of the city of Chihuahua. Grizzlies were once plains animals as well as mountain dwellers, but in their attempt to escape man they have retreated to the highest, most rugged portions of their range. Their territories and dens are generally near timberline. The dens are typically large caves or enlarged burrows.

VOICE

A low, rumbling growl combined with grunts, coughs, and barks; when angry, a ferocious bawl.

FOOD

Omnivorous. An adult bear is capable of taking elk and deer as well as domestic livestock, but his primary diet consists of berries, roots, grasses, nuts, succulent plants, fish (especially migrating salmon), garbage, and carrion.

ENEMIES

Man.

STATUS

All American grizzlies, excluding those in Alaska, are officially listed as Threatened. The Mexican subspecies is considered an Endangered Species and may be extinct. Estimates vary, but there are probably no more than 500 grizzly bears in the lower United States. The largest concentrations are found in Wyoming's Yellowstone National Park, with Glacier Park in Montana running a close second. Wyoming and Idaho have both passed moratoriums on grizzly hunting, but Montana still allows 25 bears to be killed annually—for hide and head, since few hunters take the meat. In all but these three states, the last grizzlies were destroyed by ranchers or professional hunters by 1935.

THINGS YOU SHOULD KNOW

The grizzly's demise apparently came for two reasons—his fearlessness of anything on earth, and an unequaled taste for beef on the hoof. The first resulted in a complete misunderstanding of his behavior; the second, in his slaughter. As a species, however, grizzlies are in no immediate danger of extinction, since the Alaskan and Canadian populations are stable.

Second only to the bull moose, grizzlies are the most dangerous animal in North America and should not be approached under any circumstances. Their massive bulk is coupled with a relatively small brain, and the animals are totally unpredictable, especially if hungry, injured, or (as is often the case) plagued by abscessed teeth. The worst danger of attack occurs when hikers surprise a sow with cubs. To reduce the chance of such an encounter, hikers in northern states often wear small tinkling bells. The best defense is to climb a tree, since grizzlies cannot retract their claws and climbing for them is difficult. Trying to outrun one is useless; adult bears can travel at speeds approaching 30 miles an hour over short distances.

Much of a grizzly's day is spent in pursuit of food. Individuals have been observed spending hours and huge amounts of energy digging up a single ground squirrel hole or marmot den. They love wild berries and will generally protect a favorite patch against all comers, including humans. Grizzlies sleep for extended periods during the colder months, but they do not hibernate. Their heartbeat and respiration remain normal, and they can be awakened.

Whitetail Deer
(*Odocoileus virginianus*)

ALIAS
Virginia Deer, Sonoran Deer.

IDENTIFICATION
2-3 feet high at the shoulder, weighing 50-200 pounds; generally smaller than the mule deer. The basic body color is reddish-brown in summer, and gray in winter. *The tail is brown or gray on top and white underneath; it is carried in the "plume" position when the deer is in flight.* Only males are antlered. *The antlers curve forward, and the tines are unbranched.* The whitetail's stride is a series of long, graceful bounds in contrast to the stiff-legged jump of the mule deer.

Whitetail Deer

HABITAT
Western whitetail deer, found in California, Oregon, Arizona, Idaho, Montana, and Wyoming, are transplants from larger eastern herds. The typical western habitat is deciduous forest near water, though they sometimes inhabit timbered regions. The southern sub-species (Sonoran deer) lives in the cactus and mesquite deserts of Arizona and New Mexico. Like most deer species, whitetails tend to rest during daylight hours on ridges or the fringes of clearings, feeding and watering from dusk until dawn.

VOICE
A scream when in pain or fear; females bleat to call their fawns; both sexes snort when excited.

Whitetail Deer (male)

FOOD

Leaves, shoots, buds, roots (browse), nuts, and occasionally grass. They have been observed consuming dead fish and carrion.

ENEMIES

Prolific breeders, the does commonly give birth to twins and sometimes triplets. Consequently whitetails tend to overpopulate their range and starve to death during lean winters. Western deer are not hunted seriously by man. Natural predators are coyotes, lions, and feral dogs; young are taken by bobcats and foxes.

STATUS

The Columbian whitetail, residing in Oregon and Washington, is an Endangered Species. Elsewhere whitetails are rare only because of limited range. Like many other large, edible wildlife species, whitetail populations were approaching extinction before 1900 because of constant and unrestricted hunting. With the passage of new game laws, however, the deer quickly restored themselves to stable levels.

THINGS YOU SHOULD KNOW

Whitetail deer are creatures of habit, following identical paths or feeding in favorite pastures year after year unless driven away by food shortages or heavy predation. Bucks and does generally live alone during most of the year, joining in integrated herds only during the November-December rut. Mating battles between males are ferocious but not usually fatal.

Mule Deer
(Odocoileus hemionus)

ALIAS

Mulie, Mountain Mule, Desert Deer, Rocky Mountain Burro, Gray Ghost.

IDENTIFICATION

3-4 feet high at the shoulder, weighing 100-400 pounds. The basic body color is reddish-brown in summer, gray in winter. The ears are very large and mule-like; *the tail is tipped in black and held to the haunches when the deer runs.* The gait is a stiff-legged bound. Only males are antlered. *The antlers project upward and outward with unevenly spaced, branched tines.*

HABITAT

Found from sea level to 10,000 feet in all western states, west Texas, the Dakotas, Canada's three western provinces, and the Yukon. Because of their great adaptability, mule deer exist in all types of environment and under the most rugged conditions. The general pattern for deer herds is a leisurely

Mule Deer

migration to higher altitudes during the warmer months, resting or sleeping in the daytime and feeding in valleys or high meadows during the night. Their typical habitat is open country with a view; they seldom venture into thick, overgrown timber unless frightened. Deer residing in desert regions conceal themselves in shallow arroyos or brushy areas during daylight hours. They normally do not migrate.

Mule Deer (male)

VOICE
Both sexes snort when excited; under attack or in pain, they emit a high-pitched scream; bucks sometimes bleat much like sheep.

FOOD
Herbivorous; most deer are browse animals, eating the leaves, buds, and tender shoots of green plants. During lean winters they may consume the leaves and needles of juniper, piñon, fir, and pine. Desert mule deer eat almost anything available—cactus leaves, wild fruits, yucca, wildflowers, and wild onions (desert deer habitat can usually be identified by obvious scrapes where they have pawed the ground in search of wild onions). In hard times both varieties eat grass (when this is the case, deer droppings resemble small cow pies instead of the usual hard pellet).

ENEMIES
Natural predators are mountain lions and occasionally coyotes. Bears and bobcats may take the sick and young. Hunters and automobiles destroy an estimated 400,000 mule deer annually. Where deer and humans reside in the same general area, domestic dog packs, hunting at night, kill many.

STATUS
By the end of the 19th century, mule deer populations in western America had been reduced, through overhunting, to one-tenth of their former strength. Strict new game laws combined with the establishment of wildlife refuges brought their number slowly upward. Today mule deer populations are generally stable, though the number of deer is declining slightly because of habitat destruction.

THINGS YOU SHOULD KNOW
Deer are unguligrade (toe walkers) and rank among the world's fastest mammals. They can reach a speed of 35 miles an hour, bound horizontal distances of 30 feet, and leap an 8-foot fence with no difficulty. Wide-ranging wanderers, they may travel 20 or 30 miles a

Mule Deer (female)

night to and from water.

Deer have antlers, not horns. A certain number of points on a mule deer's antlers do not necessarily tell his age. After the prime years, the older a buck becomes, the smaller his antlers are.

Throughout most of the year, males and females live alone or in bachelor herds, grouping together in loose social organization only during the September-December rut. During courtship some bucks become harem masters, leading an entourage of as many as 10 does. Others remain monogamous. Mating battles between the larger bucks are frequent but seldom end in death or injury; a few battling males may die of starvation if their antlers become permanently locked.

In January or February bucks shed their antlers and go without until a set of new, velvet-covered stubs begins to sprout in May. In early June fertile females drop from one to three odorless, well-camouflaged fawns, which are generally left in concealment during the day, joining the mother only at mealtime.

Mule deer are usually shy, but during the rut or when cornered, they can be extremely dangerous, able to kill or maim with their antlers and hooves. They do not make good pets, even when captured young.

Black-Tailed Deer
(*Odocoileus hemionus columbianus*)

ALIAS
Columbian Deer, Columbian Mule Deer, Redwood Deer.

IDENTIFICATION
3½ feet high at the shoulder, weighing 100-300 pounds; a slightly smaller, slenderer version of the western mule deer. *The body color is usually dark brown or dark gray tending to black; the underparts are whitish; the tail is totally black on top and white underneath, and is usually carried flat against the body.* The ears are wider and shorter than those of mule deer. The males have branched antlers.

HABITAT
Found on the western slope of the Cascade and Sierra Nevada mountain ranges in Washington, Oregon, and California. Typical habitat is deep forest, moist, quiet glade, or well-forested slope.

Black-Tailed Deer

VOICE
Bucks bleat; both sexes snort and emit a high-pitched squeal when frightened or in pain.

FOOD
Browse eaters; succulent plants, buds, shoots, leaves, wild berries, and nuts. They occasionally eat grass.

ENEMIES
Traditional black-tail habitat is also traditional forest fire coun-

Black-Tailed Deer (female)

try, and many deer are killed each year directly by fire and indirectly by habitat destruction and consequently starvation. Black-tails are also hunted for sport, and a few are killed by domestic dog packs and mountain lions.

STATUS
Common.

THINGS YOU SHOULD KNOW
Some zoologists consider the black-tail a subspecies of the western mule deer. In the extreme southern and western portions of black-tail range, the two frequently interbreed and the black-tail characteristics are commonly lost.

Elk
(Cervus canadensis)

ALIAS
Wapiti.

IDENTIFICATION
A very large deer, 5-6 feet high at the shoulder, weighing 400-900 pounds. The males are called bulls, and the females, cows. The basic body color is reddish-brown in summer and gray in winter. Both sexes have a distinctive yellowish rump patch and a heavy, reddish-brown mane. The legs and lower abdomen are dark brown or black. Only males have antlers; they are shed in January or February, making sex differentiation difficult until new ones begin to sprout in March.

HABITAT
Found in the Canadian Rockies and in all western states except Alaska. During the summer, typical elk habitat is brushy hillside or high meadow just below timberline. After the first snow, herds generally shift to lower altitudes, spending the cold

Elk

months in sheltered valleys or plateaus.

VOICE
Bulls bugle (a high-pitched trumpeting sound) during the fall rut; they also grunt and "mew" much like cats. Females are usually silent.

FOOD
Browse eaters; summer diet may consist of succulent plants, herbs, leaves, buds, and occasionally grass. During lean winters they often consume the bark and needles of pines, firs, or junipers. Elk lines —areas in which all vegetation has been eaten away just to the height of an elk's nose—are clues to winter range.

ENEMIES
Taking advantage of deep winter snow, which hampers an elk's mobility, grizzlies and wolf packs kill the aged or sick. Coyotes and black bears kill calves occasionally, but young elk are almost odorless and naturally camouflaged, making them difficult to find at best. Most western states allow elk hunting for sport in the fall.

STATUS
Common. Victims of extremely heavy hunting before 1900, elk were totally exterminated from many parts of the lower United States. Most American elk today are transplants from Canadian herds.

THINGS YOU SHOULD KNOW
Bulls and cows live in bachelor herds during most of the year, preferring the company and leadership of their own sex. They integrate during October, when rutting bulls become harem masters, servicing as

many as 40 cows. Mating battles between adult males are frequent and fierce, occasionally ending in death for one or both gladiators as the result of broken necks or locked antlers.

Elk can reach speeds of 30 miles an hour over short distances and can leap fences 8 or 9 feet high. They compete heavily with mule deer for browse, and generally the two species are not found in large numbers on the same range.

Elk (mature male)

Elk (male with velvet antlers)

American Moose
(Alces alces)

IDENTIFICATION

A very large deer, 5-6 feet high at the shoulder, weighing 800-1,500 pounds; the tallest land mammal in North America. Coloration varies from gray to brown. Only the males have antlers, which are normally palmate and may spread 6 to 7 feet. Both sexes have a distinguishing "bell" of skin and hair hanging from the throat. The moose's huge humped shoulders, pendulous muzzle, rubbery lips, and wide flopping ears are characteristic of no other mammal.

American Moose

American Moose (cow and calf)

HABITAT

Almost all American moose are transplants from Alaska and Canada. They are found in Washington, Idaho, Montana, Wyoming, and extreme northern Utah. Their typical habitat is heavy, coniferous forest with plenty of water available.

VOICE

To hear the mating call of a bull moose (as the old saying goes) must be an unforgettable experience indeed, since it is the cow, not the bull, that calls. The noise is an explosion of sound —a loud, harsh, "blaaaaat." Bulls grunt, cough, and groan.

FOOD

Herbivorous; leaves, sedge, and floating or submerged aquatic plants. A favorite is the waterlily. During the winter, if aquatic plants are not available, moose readily consume bark, twigs, and buds of both hardwoods and conifers.

ENEMIES

Few predators in North America have the courage or size to tackle an adult moose or even a calf if the parent is handy. Grizzlies and wolf packs are perhaps the only ones. Moose are protected in most of the lower United States, and man is not a serious enemy.

STATUS

Rare. An estimated 12,000 exist in the western states.

THINGS YOU SHOULD KNOW

At any time, but especially during the October-November rut, moose are perhaps the most dangerous mammals in North America, prone to charge anything unfamiliar. Cows with young are as unpredictable as bulls, and neither should be approached.

Much like bison, moose roll and wallow in mud, coating themselves with a thick layer as protection against biting flies and mosquitoes. They are excellent swimmers, able to paddle 10 miles or more. Capable of holding their breath for more than a minute, moose often submerge their heads entirely while feeding on the stems of succulent aquatic plants.

Rocky Mountain Bighorn Sheep
(Ovis canadensis canadensis)

ALIAS

Mountain Sheep.

IDENTIFICATION

A chunky mountain sheep, 3-4 feet high at the shoulder, weighing up to 300 pounds. The fur is heavy and coarse, varying in color from tan to deep gray; there is a distinctive white rump patch. Both sexes are horned. The ram's horns curl in a clockwise pattern and the points may be "brushed"— purposely ground off on rocks so as not to interfere with peripheral vision. The female's horns are 8-10 inches long, slender, and only slightly curved. Both sexes have slender faces but broad shoulders and rumps; the tail is short and nearly invisible.

HABITAT

Found in mountainous regions of the western states and Canada, usually above timberline. Bighorns venture where most other mammals do not— onto the steep, rocky crags of North America's most rugged mountain terrain. They are agile animals, able to leap horizontal distances of 17 feet and to move with incredible speed over crumbling talus slopes or vertical cliffs.

VOICE

Usually silent.

FOOD

Grass constitutes 90 percent of the diet. Bighorns also consume clover, wildflowers, and a wide selection of alpine browse.

ENEMIES

Two centuries ago, countless bighorns roamed the western mountain ranges. Today, estimates place the total population at about 20,000. This decline has been blamed primarily on three things: habitat destruction by domestic sheep driven into traditional bighorn pasture during the summer, heavy hunting, and disease. The most malignant is perhaps the last. Liver flukes, passed from sheep to sheep through their own droppings, and lungworms, take a tremendous toll each year.

Natural predators are few. Coyotes, lynx, and golden eagles may kill newborn lambs, but heavy predation is unlikely because bighorn parents are fiercely protective.

STATUS
Uncommon.

THINGS YOU SHOULD KNOW
Bighorn rams display their most interesting behavior during the October-December rut. Bachelors for most of the year, large rams become harem masters during this time, often collecting seven or eight females. The battles to protect their harems from younger, more aggressive intruders are fierce. Competing rams rear up on their hind legs and throw themselves forward at each other, cracking heads with incredible force. These contests of endurance and strength may continue sporadically for hours, ending only when the less dominant ram retreats. Biologists once

Rocky Mountain Bighorn Sheep (male)

(female)

thought the shock of the colliding males was absorbed by their horns, but recent studies indicate that a hind leg, lifted off the ground at the moment of impact, allows the shock to roll down the body and into the raised limb.

Bighorn sheep mature quickly, reaching their prime at the age of 5 or 6. They seldom live past 15. As a defense against predators, they depend heavily on their extraordinary vision. They can spot movement at a distance of 5 miles.

Desert Bighorn Sheep (*Ovis canadensis mexicana*)

ALIAS
Desert Sheep.

IDENTIFICATION
3-4 feet high at the shoulder, weighing an average of 200 pounds; a slenderer version of the mountain bighorn. Coloration varies from cream to gray; there is a white rump patch fading to brown near the edges; the tail is dark and short. Both sexes have horns. The ram's spiral clockwise in a wider pattern than those of the mountain bighorn, eliminating the need to "brush" the points (see under Rocky Mountain Bighorn Sheep); the female's horns are short, slender, and only slightly curved.

HABITAT
Found in desert regions of Nevada, New Mexico, Arizona, California, and the two northern states of Mexico. Typical habitat is the nearly barren slopes of desert mountain peaks, joshua or piñon forest, or rug-

Desert Bighorn Sheep (male)

ged, arid canyon country.

VOICE
A sharp snort when angry or frightened.

FOOD
Primarily grass; also cactus, cactus fruit, desert shrubs, sunflowers, and wild nuts.

ENEMIES
Natural predators are few. However, lack of water and vegetation, or heavy competition by domestic animals, sometimes decreases desert bighorn populations temporarily. Bighorns are also commonly beset by bovine diseases contracted in water holes used by domestic livestock.

STATUS
Bighorn populations decreased dramatically between 1850 and 1920 as their traditional range was confiscated by ranching interests. Today, with a few exceptions, the remaining herds live on federal wildlife refuges scattered throughout the Southwest.

THINGS YOU SHOULD KNOW
Desert bighorns inhabit excessively dry terrain and consequently sometimes go for weeks without water, extracting small amounts of moisture from the plants they eat. Occasionally, however, if no water is available at all, herds may migrate 100 miles or farther to more hospitable regions.

Only the strongest rams breed each year, a behavior that protects the dominant characteristics of a herd. The rut takes place in late summer or early fall.

Mountain Goat
(Oreamnos americanus)

ALIAS
Rocky Mountain Goat, White Goat.

IDENTIFICATION
Large mountain animals weighing 150-300 pounds, distinguished at a distance by their distinctive goat shape and shaggy white or yellowish fur. The shoulders are slightly humped; the face is slender and generally surrounded by a shaggy beard. Both sexes have slightly curved, black horns 10-12 inches long, and black hooves.

HABITAT
Found in alpine areas of the northern Rocky Mountains, the Cascades, and the Black Hills of South Dakota near Mount Rushmore. Mountain goats are cliff dwellers and are seldom seen elsewhere. Their range is usually 3-4 square miles, and even under adverse conditions, a goat will seldom leave its boundaries.

VOICE
A grunt.

FOOD
Woody stems and leaves of alpine shrubs.

ENEMIES
Snow slides probably kill more goats than all predators combined. They are also subject to pneumonia, intestinal disease, and in some areas, sport hunting by man. Occasionally golden eagles make off with the young—a difficult feat at best with nanny's dagger-sharp horns lurking nearby. A goat's white color is excellent winter camouflage, blending in amazingly well with the surrounding snow.

STATUS
Uncommon. Estimates place the goat population of the lower United States at 4,500. Probably 12,000 live in Alaska.

THINGS YOU SHOULD KNOW
The mountain goat is related to the Old World antelope and is actually not a goat at all.

Rocky Mountain Goat

Mountain goat society is dominated by the females, and the males have little responsibility. The nannies assume total care of the young and will often fight to keep the billies at a distance. The billies are polygamous, breeding in October and November with any available female. Mating battles are fierce, and death often results when one contestant is knocked from a ledge by the other.

An unusually shaped hoof—slightly concave and equipped with a spongy, non-skid bottom—permits goats to clamber across vertical cliffs even bighorn sheep would not dare to attempt.

Tough and stringy from years among the mountain crags, adult goats are hardly edible. They are hunted by man for their heads, not meat. Their carcasses are generally left to rot.

American Pronghorn (*Antilocapra americana*)

ALIAS
Antelope.

IDENTIFICATION
A distinctly deer-like animal, 3-4 feet high at the shoulder, weighing an average of 100 pounds. Coloration varies from light brown to brownish-red; the throat, chin, rump, and lower half of the abdomen are white. Bucks usually have a black throat patch, however. The legs are long and slender; the tail is short and usually tucked between the haunches. Both sexes have shiny black horns, though the female's are generally short or invisible. The male's horns are 10-14 inches long and sharply curved backward or inward at the tip, with a single prong or fork one-half to two-thirds of the way up the shaft.

HABITAT
Traditional inhabitants of the Great Plains, pronghorns typically live in sparsely timbered, rolling grassland or brushy

American Pronghorn (male)

desert. They are found throughout the western states, southern Canada, and northern Mexico. Where grass and water are plentiful, individual territories may be as small as 3 or 4 miles in diameter. Pronghorns are gregarious, and their herds may number into the hundreds.

VOICE

During the fall rut males utter a harsh, high-pitched blast not unlike the bleat of a domestic sheep. They also squeal and snort, which sounds like a human sneeze.

FOOD

Herbivorous; grass, weeds, browse, sagebrush, greasewood, alfalfa, and other grain crops.

ENEMIES

With swift flight their only defense, deep snow and barbed wire fences (which they will not jump) are indirectly a pronghorn's greatest enemies, allowing coyotes a better chance at pursuit. Overgrazing by cattle, resulting in food shortages, also takes a large annual toll.

Pronghorns are legal game in most states.

STATUS

Before 1850 American pronghorns were the only large mammals in North America with a population comparable to that of the bison. With the arrival of domestic livestock, however, they were driven from their traditional range and slaughtered by the millions for food or sport. By 1905 less than 20,000 pronghorns remained in the wild, but before total extinction could occur, laws were passed giving them badly needed protection. In many cases, however, it was necessary to transplant the animals into regions where all of them had been killed. Today, about 150,000 exist in the United States, but two subspecies, the peninsular pronghorn of Mexico and the Sonoran pronghorn of Arizona, are officially listed as Endangered Species.

THINGS YOU SHOULD KNOW

Pronghorns are probably the most unique animals in North America. They are the fastest mammal on this continent and the second fastest in the world, surpassed only by the African cheetah. Adults can reach and maintain speeds of 65 miles an hour and leap horizontal distances of 25 feet. They are the only North American mammal that evolved here and remained, rather than migrating across the Bering Land Bridge to Asia. They have true horns—modified growths of skin (cornified epithelial cells)—and not antlers like deer, but they are the only animals on earth that shed their horns each year.

Pronghorns are not a species of antelope, although that alias is used universally, even among zoologists. They have, in fact, no close relatives and are the only species of the family *Antilocapridae*.

Their tolerance of an adverse climate is amazing. Even the young can live comfortably in temperatures as high as 150 degrees or as low as −40.

Fleet of foot with exceptional vision, pronghorns have one weakness that makes a predator's life easier—curiosity. Indian hunters drew them into bow range by waving flags or skins attached to long poles. Once they sense danger, however, pronghorns contract a layer of subcutaneous rump muscles, causing the white hair to stand erect. The danger signal can be seen by other pronghorns at a distance of over a mile.

One of the most interesting facets of pronghorn behavior is their apparent pleasure at racing with automobiles. Singly or in pairs they often run alongside a moving car, speeding up or slowing down as necessary to remain abreast.

American Bison
(Bison bison)

ALIAS
Buffalo, Buffler, Buffelo.

IDENTIFICATION
10-12 feet long; 6 feet high at the shoulder; weighing 1,000-3,000 pounds. Colors vary from light brown to almost black. Both sexes have short, curving horns which are never shed. There is a distinctive hump above the shoulders. The tail is slender and usually tufted. Many bison have beards.

HABITAT
Bison once roamed nearly every part of North America, but today they are confined to refuges in Wyoming, Oregon, North and South Dakota, Oklahoma, Arizona, Montana, and Idaho. The one exception is a small, totally wild herd located near Great Slave Lake in northern Alberta, Canada. Typical bison habitat is open, grassy prairie with water nearby.

VOICE
Of all North American mammals, bison probably have the most extensive language. Their grunts, groans, squeaks, bellows, hisses, and tongue clicking all have special meaning. The alert signal, for instance, is a sharp click; an unannounced intruder standing near a herd will soon be surrounded by young protective males, clicking like crickets. Drop to one knee and they begin to groan and squeak, at the same time backing into a circular defensive position (probably an instinctive defense against wolves). Act aggressive and they will bellow (and perhaps stomp you into hamburger). Many zoologists reject the idea that bison communicate with each other in a logical vocal pattern, but references to "buffler talk" are easily found in the journals of American explorers.

FOOD
Bison once lived almost exclusively on a hearty species of plant called buffalo grass which covered the central portions of North America from Montana to Mexico. Today, because of overgrazing, buffalo grass has all but disappeared from the United States, and modern bison exist mainly on grama grass, bluegrass, and wild wheats.

ENEMIES
Biting insects; bison generally cope with this problem by acquiring a thick coating of mud or dust at "buffalo wallows." Man is their only other predator; buffalo hunts in Arizona and several other states "harvest" surplus animals.

STATUS
At the turn of the 19th century, an estimated 50 million bison of four distinct species roamed the prairies and mountains of North America. Trappers, wagon masters, army officers, and settlers told of herds 25 miles long and 50 miles wide which often took a full three days to pass a given point. But between 1800 and 1885, the four bison species—the plains bison found mainly in Kansas, the Dakotas, Montana and Wyoming; the mountain bison of Colorado; the Eastern bison; and the wood bison of the northern United States and Canada—were totally destroyed. From 1870 until 1880, probably the bloodiest period, literally millions of animals were killed each month by hunters and trappers who were paid $1.50 for each hide. In 1871 a single firm in St. Louis bought 250,000 hides. At auctions in Fort Worth, Texas, during 1873 some 200,000 a day were sold.

By 1890 concerned scientists had made an astounding discovery: of the millions of bison once so common in America, only about 300 remained, half of those in a supposedly safe refuge in Yellowstone National Park. However, before Congress enacted a law making buffalo hunting illegal in Yellowstone, hunters killed more than 100, leaving the wild herd numbering 21. Finally, in 1902, at the urging of an organization called the National Bison Society, a few animals were purchased from private herds to build up the dwindling Yellowstone band. A few years later, several federal refuges were established. Today, bison number about 35,000, but help came too late for some. The eastern and Colorado mountain species are both extinct, and the wood bison is an Endangered Species.

THINGS YOU SHOULD KNOW

Bison can sometimes be dangerous if the herd is unfamiliar with human scent. Their hearing and sense of smell are highly developed, but their eyesight is poor, and a testy old bull might trample an intruder before realizing his victim was harmless. If one is cautious, however, meandering about in a bison herd is an enjoyable experience and far safer than riding with a New York taxi driver.

Bison rut during early summer, and bulls who defeat less experienced competitors in head-butting contests may take harems of 20 cows. Throughout the year bison are gregarious, and only large, irascible, nonbreeding bulls live by themselves.

American Bison

Wild Burro
(Equus asinus)

ALIAS

Wild Donkey, Wild Ass, Jackass.

IDENTIFICATION

The wild burro closely resembles the domestic burro; it weighs 300-400 pounds. Coloration encompasses the entire range of normal horse colors, but many wild burros are dusty gray with black mane and tail. A dark, narrow, shoulder-to-shoulder stripe usually bisects the back.

HABITAT

Typical habitat is desert or rugged canyon country. Wild burro populations are relatively few in number; their primary American ranges are as follows: the south end of Grand Canyon National Park near the Colorado River; along the Colorado River near Lake Havasu, Arizona; Death Valley, California; near Las Vegas, in southern Nevada; Bandolier National Monument, near Los Alamos, New Mexico; and Three Rivers,

Wild Burro (female)

New Mexico, near White Sands National Monument.

VOICE
A bray.

FOOD
Whatever is handy is eaten; cactus, yucca, weeds, brush, mesquite, and grass are the most common foods.

ENEMIES
Man.

STATUS
Never as common as wild horses, burros have suffered the same treatment; large numbers in the past have been trapped for dog food or shot because of competition with domestic cattle. The Wild Horse and Burro Act now protects those living on public land. Many of the remaining herds, even though they reside on federal reserves, can still be destroyed legally (and commonly are) as individual government agencies deem necessary. The best estimates place the total wild burro population in the United States at 20,000.

THINGS YOU SHOULD KNOW
America's wild burros are probably direct descendants of 15 burros brought from Spain to Santa Fe, New Mexico, in 1631 as a gift to the explorer Oñate from the Spanish king.

Wild Horse
(Equus caballus)

ALIAS
Mustang, Spanish Mustang, Spanish Barb, Broom Tail, Bang-Tail.

IDENTIFICATION
A small, slender horse closely resembling domestic breeds; the mane and tail are usually long and unkempt, and the hooves unshod. Coloration varies from palomino to black; the most unique coloration is the Medicine Hat, a black-on-white pinto with dark spots around the eyes.

HABITAT
Wild horse herds exist in all western states except Washington and Montana. The largest, containing about half the total number, is found in Nevada. Typical habitat is rugged, broken desert country far from human habitation.

FOOD
Wild grasses.

ENEMIES
Man.

STATUS
As late as 1850, several million wild horses ranged across the western United States from Texas to Oregon, unmolested except for Plains Indian subcultures, which used them for transport and occasionally for intertribal war. As civilization expanded westward, however, wild horse herds began competing with domestic livestock for water and grass. Ranchers were quick to intervene. Thousands upon thousands of wild horses were either shot and left on the plains to rot or rounded up and sold for dog food. Another blow came in 1934, when Congress passed the Taylor Grazing Act, giving control of 143 million acres of public land to ranchers. Most was immediately fenced, and wild horses that had escaped earlier slaughter were now rounded up and destroyed. The wild horse herds remaining today are protected by the federal Wild Horse and Burro Act, passed in 1971, but poachers have de-

Wild Horse

creased their population to less than 17,000.

THINGS YOU SHOULD KNOW

The horse is a North American native which initially appeared 50 million years ago as a small, four-toed plains animal called eohippus. Later, when the formation of the Bering Land Bridge connected North America with Asia, eohippus migrated and became extinct on this continent. His descendants returned to North America, first with Columbus, then later with Spanish conquistadors in the 16th century. The question of how horses came to be wild still baffles historians. The most prevalent theory is that a few escaped from Spanish haciendas in northern Mexico, crossed into Texas, and over a period of two centuries, migrated to the north and west.

4/

AQUATIC MAMMALS

Muskrat
(*Ondatra zibethica*)

ALIAS
Marsh Rabbit.

IDENTIFICATION
A thickly furred, rat-like mammal, 1½-2 feet long, including a *long, hairless, vertically flattened tail*. The basic body color is dark brown or black. The eyes and ears are small, and the hind feet partially webbed. Muskrats are seldom seen on land.

HABITAT
Found from sea level to 9,000 feet in all western states, Canada, and Alaska. Typical habitat is aquatic—marsh, swamp, slow-moving river, or lake. Muskrat habitat can generally be identified by clusters of freshly chewed reeds or cattails along the bank. The den may be an elaborate subterranean burrow with two or more entrances, or a rambling surface dwelling constructed of sticks, weeds, or roots.

Muskrat

VOICE
A rapid chattering or teeth-gnashing when angry or excited; also snarls and squeaks.

FOOD
Omnivorous; cattails, succulent plants, roots, bark, fish, crayfish, frogs, snails, and carrion. Muskrats sometimes practice cannibalism when another member of their species has been killed.

ENEMIES
Natural predators are foxes, minks, raccoons, predacious fish (mainly northern pike), and birds of prey. Muskrats are America's primary source of fur and are heavily trapped by man.

STATUS
Common.

THINGS YOU SHOULD KNOW
Six million muskrat pelts—each bringing about $7.50 to the trapper—are sold annually to furriers in the United States, to be used in the manufacture of coats, collars, handbags, and garment trim. Muskrat carcasses are sometimes sold to restaurants and offered to the public as Marsh Rabbit. Muskrat trapping is not a humane practice. Steel-jawed traps are anchored a few inches under water in a feed-bed of cattails or reeds by means of a long wire or chain. When a muskrat bumps the trap with its foot, the trap snaps closed. In shock and surprise, the muskrat's impulse is to dive, entangling the chain on aquatic plants. Generally drowning results. If the animal somehow escapes this watery death, its natural inclination is self-amputation of the trapped limb.

When aquatic mammals get their fur soiled, only a small amount of insulating air is trapped by the underpelt, and the cold seeps through. Consequently muskrats are intensely fastidious, grooming their fur several times a day.

Beaver
(Castor canadensis)

IDENTIFICATION
America's largest rodent, 3-4 feet in length, weighing about 70 pounds on the average. The basic color is deep, rich brown or black; the legs and ears are short; the hind feet are webbed; the tail is wide, flat, and scaly. Beavers are easily distinguished from muskrat or otter in the water by their large size and broad, flat heads.

HABITAT
Found from sea level to 9,000 feet throughout the West (including Alaska and Canada) along waterways, lakes, permanent ponds, and even some irrigation ditches. Typical beaver habitat is a small, easily dammed mountain stream. Beavers are adaptable creatures, however, needing only water and a healthy supply of trees or brush to survive.

Lodge beavers, those constructing dams and large houses of sticks, are the most commonly observed in western America. Some beavers, however, den in burrows beneath river banks or large windfalls and do not erect dams. In either case beaver habitat can usually be identified by piles of cleanly stripped branches lying at the water's edge or many fallen trees. Most beavers create scent mounds—large piles of mud and grass that have been sprayed with urine or castorium (musk) to warn migrating beavers away. The scent mounds are not easily missed.

VOICE
An occasional bark, hiss, or squeal; the most common utterance is a soft "mew."

FOOD
Vegetarian; the diet consists primarily of the soft, chewable inner bark (cambium) of aspen, pine, fir, beech, cottonwood, or maple trees, though occasionally the entire tree is consumed. Lodge beavers construct reserve "food beds" of uneaten branches and limbs which are usually stuck into a pond's muddy bottom. They are eaten during the winter when fresh

food is difficult to obtain.

ENEMIES

Natural predators are few; coyotes, bears, and bobcats probably kill an occasional kit; some adults are crushed when the very tree they are gnawing on falls the wrong way. Others may starve during the winter if their pond and lodge freeze solid, cutting off access to the food bed. North American trappers still catch almost 200,000 beavers a year; their pelts bring $30 to $70 each.

STATUS

Between 1750 and 1830 the pursuit of beavers by French trappers and voyageurs was responsible for much of the interior exploration of North America. With an excellent market for pelts (used to make gentlemen's hats) in Europe, canoe-borne adventurers found exploration and trapping a paying proposition. By 1830 millions of furs a year were being shipped to markets in London. Even when silk was discovered in 1832 and beaver hats were no longer in vogue,

Beaver (female)

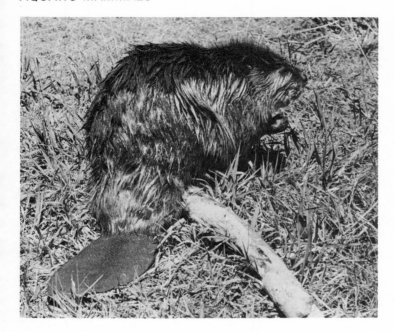

the pelts were still in demand for capes, colars, and trim. Only when beaver populations were approaching extinction, probably around 1870, did the pressure lift. Today, because of organized transplanting, beavers are relatively common, but the countless millions that once inhabited North America are gone forever.

THINGS YOU SHOULD KNOW
Beavers construct dams for several important reasons. The foremost is personal protection. The aquatic environment created by a sturdy dam is the sole defense these slow, deliberate animals have against predators. Dams and the ponds created by them also act as storage centers for winter food supplies. Most lodges are constructed in deep water so that the underwater entrance is well below the winter ice line. Then, even if the pond's surface is frozen, foraging beavers can move freely from lodge to food bed. Beaver dams are usually shored up in the fall so as to raise the pond's water level, thereby making it less likely that the lodge entrance will freeze.

An adult beaver can remain submerged for 15 minutes. The wide, flat tail is used primarily as a rudder, but it may also be used (with long vertical strokes) as an aid to rapid swimming under water. On land the tail is used as a third leg, propping the animal up as he gnaws at a tree. *It is not used to carry or pack mud.* Mud used in building dams is transported between the forelegs and chest, and packed into place with the front paws.

American River Otter
(*Lutra canadensis*)

ALIAS
Land Otter, Canada Otter.

IDENTIFICATION
A long, slender aquatic weasel, 3-5 feet long, including a thick, blunt, heavily furred tail; the average weight is 35-40 pounds. The fur color is rich, chocolate brown with light gray underparts and throat; the head is bullet-shaped with long, prominent whiskers; all four feet are webbed.

HABITAT
Depending on water for existence, otters can be found in most of the larger lakes, marshes, and rivers of the West. They do not inhabit the Southwest, although undocumented reports place them on the lower Colorado and Rio Grande rivers in Arizona and New Mexico. Otter dens may be enlarged muskrat holes or cavities in a river bank; the entrances are generally under water. In some regions, females den beneath "wigwams" of

American River Otter (male)

reeds or cattails. Individual territories often cover 75 miles of shoreline. Much like beavers, otters construct scent mounds called spraints to notify others that the territory is occupied.

VOICE
Otters have an extensive vocabulary. Most common is a chirp, squeal, or screech; they may hiccup or chuckle when at play and hiss when angry.

FOOD
The otter's metabolism requires food often and in great quantities. Voracious eaters, they consume fish, clams, mussels, crayfish, frogs, snails, reptiles, insects, ducks, and rodents, all with the delightful gusto of a hungry child.

ENEMIES
Pollution is perhaps the greatest threat to American otters, since industrial wastes and collective poisons are destroying their food supply. The destruction of wetlands is another danger. According to a national survey, otter and other aquatic animal habitats are being over-taken by industry at the alarming rate of 2,000 acres a day. Otter pelts have always commanded an excellent price in fur markets, and currently about 11,000 otters are trapped each year in North America.

STATUS
Rare.

THINGS YOU SHOULD KNOW
Otters are best described as clowns—playful, mischievous, and full of fun. One of their favorite pastimes is sliding down chutes made of mud or snow on their stomachs. They wrestle, play games, and amuse themselves for hours with seemingly boring items like a dead fish or a pebble.

Perhaps the best swimmers of all American mammals, otters can remain submerged for up to 4 minutes. To conserve oxygen while under water, their heartbeat slows to about 20 beats per second and their nostrils and ears are automatically shut off by flaps of skin. Aided by river currents, an adult otter can swim more than a quarter of a mile under water.

Sea Otter
(*Enhydra lutris*)

ALIAS
Sea Beaver.

IDENTIFICATION
A robust, aquatic sea mammal, 3-4 feet long; the average weight is 70 pounds. The fur is lustrous dark brown, slightly mottled by long silver guard hairs. Mature adults usually have light-colored faces with white whiskers. The hind feet are wide and fully flippered; the tail is short, thick, and horizontally flattened.

HABITAT
North American sea otters exist only along a rugged strip of California shoreline near Monterey and on Alaska's Aleutian Islands. Typical habitat is a rocky coastline with protected bays and kelp beds close by. Sea otters generally remain within 200 yards of shore and prefer water less than 150 feet deep. They sleep, feed, breed, and give birth in the ocean, seldom if ever venturing onto land. Usually gregarious, they

Sea Otter

live in families called pods.

VOICE
An infrequent bark, squeal, or growl.

FOOD
Carnivorous; 95 percent of their diet consists of sea urchins, crabs, or mussels, and a single otter may consume 2½ tons of food each year. The nose is blunted so that the teeth can be used to pry shellfish from rocks, and the teeth themselves are rounded for crushing mollusk shells.

ENEMIES
Killer Whales.

STATUS
From 1737 until the early 1800's, sea otters were the most sought-after furbearers on earth. A single pelt brought as much as $1000 in the European fur market; consequently, by the beginning of the 19th century the animal was all but extinct. Then, during a short respite between 1800 and 1860, unrestricted hunting halted and the otters slowly but steadily increased their population. As they multiplied, however, the hunters returned, and by 1911 sea otters were thought to be extinct in the United States and on the edge of extinction elsewhere.

Then, much to the surprise of American zoologists, an otter pod was discovered off the California coast near Carmel in 1935. Under limited protection from the government, a stable population established itself once again. Today sea otters are totally protected; even to own a strip of otter fur is a federal offense. The California population is estimated at 1,400 animals and steadily growing. But in the last few years, commercial fishermen have begun to complain that the otters destroy both abalone and sea urchins in numbers large enough to affect the annual commercial harvest. At present, California officials are attempting to wrest control of sea otters from the federal government so that the animals can be harvested to avoid the hazards of overpopulation.

THINGS YOU SHOULD KNOW
Adult otters in search of food dive to 150-foot depths and often remain submerged for 5 minutes. They generally feed three times daily—in the early morning, at noon, and in the late evening—but a snack or two between meals is not uncommon. The use of tools in their feeding behavior is unique; beneath the surface, they may use a large rock to extract mollusks from rocks. Then, once on the surface, the otters roll onto their backs, prop the rock on their stomachs, and using it as an avil, rap their victim until its shell cracks. If the entree is a crab, it is torn

limb from limb and consumed with the apparent delight of a small boy eating fried chicken. At dinner's end, a 360 degree roll drops the leftovers overboard.

Between meals, otter pods sleep or sun, rolling themselves in long strands of kelp until only their feet and heads are showing (a behavior known as "rafting"). The pose often resembles that of lounging humans—feet crossed, front paws folded behind the head or on the chest, and eyes closed.

Since they have no insulating blubber for warmth, otters must keep their fur clean and free from sludge. Several times a day they give themselves a thorough grooming with their long front claws.

Sea Lions

IDENTIFICATION
Two principal western species are described below.

Northern Sea Lion (*Eumetopias jubata*). A large aquatic mammal, 10-12 feet long, weighing 1,200-2,000 pounds. Females are slightly smaller. The basic body color varies from yellow to brown, turning darker when the animal is wet. Typical habitat is the Pacific coast from Alaska south to Oregon and sometimes into northern California.

California Sea Lion (*Zalophus californianus*). Smaller than the northern species; 5-8 feet long, weighing 500-800 pounds. The basic body color varies from tan to black. *Males sometimes have a high, crested forehead.* Both species spend much of their time sunning or sleeping on rocky islands or causeways. They are gregarious, usually congregating in groups of 30 or more. During the rut, males may take harems of 15 or 20 females.

California Sea Lion (female)

VOICE
California sea lions are vocal; they yelp, holler, growl, honk, and bark. Northern sea lions roar *but never bark*.

FOOD
Carnivorous; a sea lion's diet consists of squid and small fish, usually taken after dark. Adults may consume 12-15 pounds per day.

ENEMIES
Killer whales and large sharks; man is not a serious predator.

STATUS
Common. The best estimates place the total sea lion population at about 300,000.

THINGS YOU SHOULD KNOW
The trained "seals" so commonly on public display are usually California sea lions. They readily adapt to captivity and can be trained easily.

Before the widespread use of plastics and other synthetic materials, sea lions were hunted heavily, especially by northern Indian tribes. Nearly every part of their body was used: the flesh for food, hides for shelter and boat covers, organs and genitals for medicine and aphrodisiacs. Even the whiskers were used—as pipe cleaners.

5/

PRIMATES

Bigfoot
(Homo gigantis)

ALIAS
Sasquatch, Omah.

IDENTIFICATION
A large hominid, 8-10 feet tall, weighing 500-1,000 pounds; the body fur color is brown or black; the forehead is high; the mouth is large; the nose, flattened. The animal is generally seen walking upright. He emits a powerful, unpleasant odor. His tracks are 2-3 inches deep, 18 inches long, 8 inches wide, and may have either 3 or 5 toes.

HABITAT
Found in the coastal mountains of California, Oregon, Washington, and British Columbia. Typical Bigfoot habitat is moist, temperate mountain country with water nearby. Recent sightings have placed Bigfoot in Tuolumne County, California; the Lower Rogue River Canyon, Oregon; Siuslaw National Forest, Oregon; and The Dalles, Oregon. The species is thought to be nomadic and nocturnal. Bigfoot dens are probably in caves.

VOICE
A deep-pitched series of grunts, squeals, and roars, oriental in pattern, without the use of a long E.

FOOD
Omnivorous; roots, berries, wild nuts, small rodents, fish.

ENEMIES
Probably subject to pneumonia, ticks, fleas, and intestinal disorders.

STATUS
Rare. The total United States Bigfoot population is thought to be less than 200.

THINGS YOU SHOULD KNOW
First identified by western Indian tribes more than a century ago, Bigfoot has since baffled thousands of investigators, who have attempted to track him down. Many scientists, in fact, remain skeptical about the animal's existence, arguing that if an American primate did exist, hard evidence—a live specimen or at least a carcass would have been discovered by now. However, wild animals with well-developed senses easily remain unseen if they wish, and the remains of many wildlife species are seldom, if ever, discovered in the wild. It is not unlikely that an unknown primate species might bury its dead or dispose of them in some other way such as cannibalism.

Recently, investigators have organized a clearinghouse for information concerning Bigfoot, and any sightings or other evidence should be reported immediately to the Bigfoot Information Center, Box 632, The Dalles, Oregon. Telephone (503) 298-5877.

6/

BIRDS OF PREY

Notes on Birds of Prey

For the sake of convenience, the predacious birds discussed in this book may be divided into five general categories—owls, falcons, hawks or buteos, eagles, and vultures. With the exception of the burrowing variety, owls are night hunters, resting or sleeping the daylight away in some dark cavity or nest. Generally they are large, well-rounded birds, with eyes set on the front of the head. Their feet and legs are usually feathered, and some species have ear tufts. The wings are broad and heavy. Falcons are the smallest birds of prey, streamlined and fast-flying, with slender, pointed wings and narrow tails. Most have special physical adaptations that allow unusual speed in flight. The hawks or buteos are day hunters. Their bodies are generally heavy with broad tails and wings. Eagles, of course, are the largest American birds of prey. Their bills and talons are extremely heavy and powerful. Vultures are the carrion eaters, doomed because of their physical characteristics to consume the rotting flesh of other animals.

However, even when one has a working knowledge of these five categories, predacious birds are perhaps the most difficult of all North American wild animals to identify in the field. Cautious by nature, they have come to fear man, seldom allowing intruders to approach near enough for more than a quick glance. In addition, their colorations are so variable that dependable identifying characteristics are few. Not only do immature birds differ greatly from adults, but young hawks and eagles quite often resemble each other, no matter what their particular species.

The observer's initial glance, when attempting to identify predacious birds, should be a general one, allowing the eye to pinpoint any characteristic that definitely marks the bird as a certain species. For example, a pure white head and tail on a large soaring bird would indicate it was a bald eagle. Or, a white-tipped tail on a dark, medium-sized hawk probably means the animal is a Harris' hawk.

If no single identifying characteristic can be observed, consider the bird's coloration, shape, and location. Burrowing owls, for instance, are small, rounded birds, usually brown or gray, seen most often on the ground in desert or plains areas. A small, slender falcon hunting in a cultivated field is probably a sparrow hawk. If all else fails, combine every possible bit of evidence—coloration, habitat, size, shape, and voice (if heard)—and hope for the best. Remember, however, that where predacious birds are concerned, nature has no absolutes. Coloration, size, and shape may vary with the age of the bird or season of the year. And since most birds of prey migrate with changing seasons, a particular species might easily be observed in a totally alien location. Even experts are wrong 50 percent of the time.

In certain regions, nest construction and egg color can be added to the list of identifying characteristics, but observers should not approach a nest unless absolutely necessary. Not only is it dangerous, since some birds are capable of removing an ear or clump of hair with their talons, but in many cases an approach might frighten the young from the nest. They probably could not make their way back and would soon fall prey to vigilant carnivores.

Burrowing Owl
(Speotyto cunicularia)

ALIAS
Ground Owl, Digger Owl.

IDENTIFICATION
A small, well-rounded, diurnal owl, 8-10 inches high, with a short, stubby tail. The body color is usually spotted brown; the legs are extremely long and only lightly feathered. The flight pattern is rapid and undulating; flights are seldom more than 50 yards long and a few seconds in duration, usually at an altitude of 5-8 feet off the ground. A burrowing owl is commonly seen "bobbing and bowing" nervously as he watches an intruder.

HABITAT
Found in all western states, Canada, and Mexico. Typical habitat is open grassland, plain, and in many cases, desert. The nest is usually an abandoned badger or prairie dog hole lined with horse or cow manure.

Burrowing Owl

EGGS
6-9; dirty white.

VOICE
A soft and very rapid "whit-whit-whit."

FOOD
Small rodents, snakes, lizards, large beetles, and grasshoppers; the young occasionally practice cannibalism.

ENEMIES
Burrow-dwelling carnivores—mainly badgers and skunks—raid their nests for eggs and young; adults are sometimes killed by man as pests or when mistaken in flight for game birds.

Burrowing Owl

Burrowing Owl roosting

STATUS

Poison campaigns directed at prairie dogs have also decimated burrowing owl populations, since the two often share the same range. Before 1920, "owl towns" many miles across were common. Today, these small predacious birds are protected by federal law. They are rare, but not endangered.

THINGS YOU SHOULD KNOW

The burrowing owl's eyes are located on the front of the head, allowing binocular vision much like that of humans, though many times more powerful. Hence an owl must twist its neck to see behind, whereas other birds of prey, whose eyes are on the sides of the head, can see in all directions at once.

Some experts contend that burrowing owls migrate to warmer climates during the winter. Others think they simply "hole up" in burrows during heavy snows. The latter theory seems more likely, since burrowing owls are hoarders, storing piles of food in their nests.

Usually gentle and retiring, burrowing owls have been known to attack humans attempting to destroy their nests.

American Barn Owl (*Tyto alba*)

ALIAS

Monkey-Faced Owl, Spook Owl.

IDENTIFICATION

A large, nocturnal owl, 15-20 inches high, *with large, white, heart-shaped facial disks*. The basic body color is brownish-yellow with pale, almost white underparts. The flight patterns are graceful, swift, and moth-like.

Barn Owl Facial Features

HABITAT

Found in prairie regions or open country, often in the close vicinity of man. The nest is usually an abandoned badger or coyote burrow liberally carpeted with fur pellets (balls of undigested fur, bones, and skulls of their prey which are recurrently disgorged), or a quiet corner in an unused building.

EGGS

7-9; usually dull white.

VOICE

A hiss or rapid clicking of the bill when anxious or surprised; in flight, an "ick-ick-ick-ick."

FOOD

Small rodents, insects, and occasionally poultry.

ENEMIES

Mistakenly accused of killing large numbers of upland game birds, barn owls are often shot as pests. Natural predators are great horned owls and prairie falcons.

American Barn Owl

STATUS
Common.

THINGS YOU SHOULD KNOW
Since a single hunting owl with nesting young may take 10 to 15 mice a night, barn owls are extremely beneficial to farmers. Their ears are so sensitive that they can capture prey by their hearing alone. However, their vision is also extraordinary: a barn owl can hit a rapidly moving target by the equivalent light of a candle 1,100 feet away.

Glaring from the darkened corners of abandoned buildings, the spooky, heart-shaped facial disks of barn owls have given rise to many haunted-house stories.

Great Horned Owl
(Bubo virginianus)

ALIAS
Hoot Owl, Cat Owl, Winged Tiger, Night Owl.

IDENTIFICATION
The largest "eared" owl found in North America; 18-24 inches high; the ear tufts are 1½-2 inches long. The basic body color is overall gray, splotched with brown and white; there is a conspicuous white collar just beneath the bill. The feet are light-colored and fully feathered; the eyes are large and golden. The flight patterns can best be described as shadowy.

HABITAT
Found in all western states, Alaska, Canada, and Mexico. Typical habitat is woody, hilly terrain near water, though great horned owls inhabit almost any type of environment. The nest is generally a feather-lined cavity in a cliff, sandy bank, or tree, or occasionally on the ground. Individual territories are usually large, but great horned owls are such effective

Great Horned Owl

hunters that nocturnal game populations are often quickly exhausted. Consequently, they must change territories frequently.

EGGS
2; white.

VOICE
A mysterious and subtle "hooot" or "hoo-hoo." Females may "erk" and "ank." When frightened or surprised, both sexes hiss loudly and pop their bills.

FOOD
Voracious feeders, great horned owls normally eat anything that walks, flies, swims, or crawls if it is small enough to kill. Their talons are extremely powerful, and they have been known to attack coyotes, porcupines, dogs, cats, skunks (they are apparently unscathed by the skunk's powerful emission), and even light-colored fur hats worn by humans.

ENEMIES
In heavily trapped areas, owls are sometimes caught while attempting to eat bait meant for coyotes or other fur bearers. They are also commonly harassed by crows, hawks, and little gray birds over territorial disputes. The primary enemy, however, is the automobile, which kills thousands each year.

STATUS
Common; protected by federal law.

THINGS YOU SHOULD KNOW
Great horned owls are night hunters, swift, silent, and deadly to small forest animals. Their large golden eyes are 100 times as powerful as those of humans and are equipped with a cleansing membrane that washes the eye with each blink. The eardrums are larger than those of any other bird.

Mating owls take part in unique courting rituals which include bowing, stroking, touching bills, and presenting a gift (usually a dead rat or mouse) to the prospective mate. The females lay their eggs in January, a month earlier than most other birds of prey. Adult owls dislike leaving a nest with eggs and may fly directly at an intruder in an attempt to drive him away.

Great Horned Owl

Sparrow Hawk
(Falco sparverius)

ALIAS
American Kestrel, Mouse Hawk, Grasshopper Hawk.

IDENTIFICATION
A small falcon less than 12 inches long with a wingspread of 1½-2 feet. *The basic body color is reddish-brown* with a light-colored stomach and chest; *the head is crowned with dull red; the face is barred with twin black vertical stripes* (eye spots); the tail is long, slender, reddish-brown on top and banded black beneath. *Sparrow hawks are commonly observed hovering on rapidly beating wings while searching the ground below for prey.*

HABITAT
Found from sea level to 12,000 feet in all western states, Alaska, Canada, and Mexico. Typical habitat is open prairie, desert, meadow, or farmland. Heavily wooded regions are usually shunned. The nest is usually a small twig platform in a tree, cliff face, or unused

Sparrow Hawk

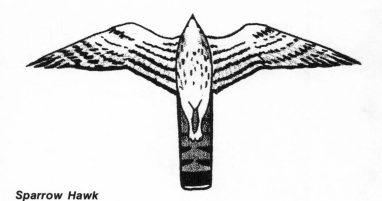

Sparrow Hawk

woodpecker hole.

EGGS
4-5; pinkish-white.

VOICE
A rapid, high-pitched "quee-quee-quee," interpreted by some ornithologists as "killy-killy-killy."

FOOD
About 80 percent of a sparrow hawk's diet consists of small mammals, lizards, and insects. The name sparrow hawk refers to the bird's relatively small size, not food choice, though small birds are sometimes caught and killed.

ENEMIES
These small, fast birds are commonly affected by pesticides used to control insects, which may result in thin eggshells and premature young. They are also killed in large numbers by automobiles.

STATUS
Common; protected by federal law.

THINGS YOU SHOULD KNOW

Unlike most diurnal predacious birds, sparrow hawks sometimes nest in holes or cavities—often abandoned woodpecker holes high in a tree. They are extremely protective of their small territories, fiercely attacking and driving off intruding birds several times their size. Fast and agile fliers, they are able to cruise at 25 miles an hour. Their vision is excellent. A lubricant coats the eyes to filter out haze or bright glare, and black eyespots beneath the eyes also absorb glare.

Peregrine Falcon
(*Falco peregrinus*)

ALIAS
Duck Hawk.

IDENTIFICATION
A medium-sized, fast-flying falcon, 15-20 inches long with a wingspread averaging 3 feet. The basic body color is slate-gray; the underparts are lightly splotched or barred with brown; the head is usually black. *There is a distinctive black patch (mustache) below the eyes*. The wings are long, slender and pointed. The wing-beats are rapid and shallow.

HABITAT
Probably less than 50 nesting pairs of peregrines exist in the western United States, most of them in the Rocky Mountains. There is a relatively stable population in Alaska, however. The nest is almost always located on a high, unreachable cliff face, and mating pairs usually return to the same nesting site year after year. Any sightings should be immediately reported to the nearest office

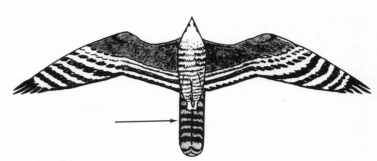

Peregrine Falcon

of the U.S. Fish and Wildlife Service.

EGGS
3-4; pinkish-white, with brownish-red speckles.

VOICE
Usually silent.

FOOD
Peregrines are bird eaters, preying mainly on jays, woodpeckers, quail, ducks, pigeons, and small songbirds. Most prey is captured in flight. Perhaps the swiftest-flying birds on earth, peregrines may soar 1,000 feet above the ground while hunting, then "stoop" at speeds approaching 200 miles an hour. Death for the unlucky victim usually results from shock. The prey is generally plucked daintily before being eaten.

ENEMIES
Pesticides.

STATUS
Endangered.

THINGS YOU SHOULD KNOW
More than any other bird of prey, peregrines are affected by pesticides meant for crop-destroying insects. Since their primary diet consists of insect-eating birds, peregrines re-

Peregrine Falcon

ceive the pesticides through ingestion; once in the body, the chemicals reduce the level of calcium, resulting in thin eggshells that will not support the weight of a nesting parent.

Male peregrines (tiercels) give dramatic displays of aerial acrobatics during mating season. They also protect the female and nest fiercely against all intruders.

In part, the peregrine's rapid flight is made possible by a specially adapted nostril structure which breaks up the air and allows breathing at high speeds. Consisting of small fins and rods, the complex structure causes air to whirl so that it takes only a tiny effort on the part of the bird to breathe.

Prairie Falcon
(Falco mexicanus)

IDENTIFICATION
A small, light-brown falcon, 16-20 inches long with a wingspread up to 3½ feet. The underparts are white with brown bars; the wings are long and pointed. *In flight, prairie falcons may be distinguished by large black patches where the wings attach to the body.* Their flight is rapid, with shallow wingbeats.

HABITAT
Found in most of the western states except along the Pacific coast. Typical habitat is prairie, open desert, or rugged foothill country. The nest is generally located on a sunny cliff face.

EGGS
2-3; white with tiny brown speckles.

VOICE
A "kic-kic-kic-kic."

FOOD
Small rodents, ground birds, and all types of flying birds.

ENEMIES
Pesticides, territorial destruction, and harassment by humans.

Prairie Falcon

Prairie Falcon

STATUS
Rare; protected by federal law.

THINGS YOU SHOULD KNOW
Greatly affected by pesticides, prairie falcons have undergone dramatic losses in the past few decades. They also suffer from any human presence near their nests. State and federal officials responsible for the prairie falcon's survival now keep nesting sites secret to prevent human intrusion.

Harris' Hawk
(*Parabuteo unicinctus*)

IDENTIFICATION
A medium-sized hawk, 20-22 inches long with a wingspread of about 4 feet. The basic body color is usually dark brown or gray, with reddish spots on the thighs and wings. *The tail is dark with a distinctive white tip.* There is also a distinctive white patch at the base of the rump.

HABITAT
Found mainly in the desert country or mesquite flats of Texas, New Mexico, Arizona, Nevada, and southern California, and into Mexico. The nest is generally a tightly knit platform of sticks lined with soft grass, constructed near the ground in low bushes.

EGGS
Usually 3; white or pale blue.

VOICE
A harsh "kreeeek" or "krawwwwwk." In flight, a high-pitched "queeee-ger."

Harris' Hawk

FOOD
Small mammals, rodents, lizards, snakes, slower species of waterfowl, small birds, and carrion.

ENEMIES
Primarily man; coyotes and bobcats often invade the low-built nests to capture the young.

STATUS
Common.

THINGS YOU SHOULD KNOW
A Harris' hawk's flight is generally a slow, buoyant glide, almost as if the bird has nowhere to go and all the time in the world to get there. When prey is sighted, however, the Harris' hawk suddenly changes into a swift, competent predator, diving and striking with almost the fearful speed of the prairie or peregrine falcon. Unfortunately, these birds are seemingly unafraid of man, so they are quite often shot from their perches.

Harris' Hawk (dark phase)

Rough-Legged Hawk
(*Buteo lagopus*)

ALIAS
American Rough-Leg.

IDENTIFICATION
A slender, medium-sized hawk, 20-23 inches long with a wingspread of 4-4½ feet. The basic body color may be white with many large brown splotches, or almost totally black. *The rump, in either color phase, is distinctly marked by a white patch, easily seen in flight.* The tail is short, light-colored, and marked with a wide dark band near the tip. *The legs are fully feathered.* In flight, the wings are broad and usually marked with black patches at the wrists.

HABITAT
Found in New Mexico, Texas, northern Arizona, California, Oregon, and Washington. Typical habitat is prairie or open country, usually near water. The nest is constructed on a small, rocky ledge or in a deep hole in a river bank.

EGGS
3-4; dingy white with dark splotches.

VOICE
A loud screech.

Rough-Legged Hawk

Rough-Legged Hawk (light phase)

FOOD

The rough-legged hawk is an excellent mouse catcher, able to hover on its rapidly flashing wings while waiting for the prey to show itself ("stilling"). It is one of the few large hawks to exhibit this type of behavior. Its feet are small, adapted to catching tiny rodents, and it seldom takes larger prey. Rough-legs do not eat snakes, since their feathered legs do not protect them from snakebite. Most reptile-eating birds have naked, scaly legs.

ENEMIES

Man.

STATUS

Common.

THINGS YOU SHOULD KNOW

Probably the most nocturnal of hawks, rough-legs usually hunt during late evening, perhaps because their primary prey, field mice, are more active during that time.

Ferruginous Hawk
(Buteo regalis)

ALIAS
Ferruginous Rough-Legged Hawk, Rough-Legged Buzzard.

IDENTIFICATION
A slender, light-colored hawk, 20-25 inches long with a wing-spread of 4½ feet. The shoulders and back are reddish-brown; the breast is generally white or tan. *The legs are fully feathered and usually dark; in flight the dark leg feathers are highly visible.* The tail is light-colored and unbanded.

HABITAT
Found in southern Canada and most of the western United States, south to New Mexico and Texas. Typical habitat is desert or plain, quite often where water is not abundant. The nest is usually constructed in a tree and sometimes on a cliff face.

EGGS
4; white with brown spots.

VOICE
In flight, a shrieking "kreeee."

FOOD
Small rodents—rats, mice, gophers, and ground squirrels.

Ferruginous Hawk (light phase)

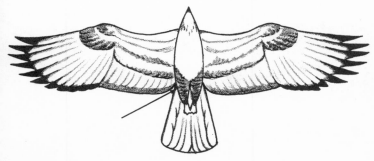

Ferruginous Hawk

ENEMIES
Man.

STATUS
Common.

THINGS YOU SHOULD KNOW
Like rough-legged hawks, ferruginous hawks do not eat snakes, since their feathered legs offer little protection from a poisonous bite. They occasionally eat carrion, however; consequently they are often sighted near carcasses of domestic livestock and shot by ranchers who mistakenly think they are responsible for the livestock's death.

Swainson's Hawk
(*Buteo swainsoni*)

ALIAS
Swainson's Buzzard.

IDENTIFICATION
A medium-sized brown and white hawk, 18-20 inches long with a wingspread of 4 feet. The throat and underparts are white with *a wide reddish band across the chest* (the band may sometimes be broken into spots). The wings are dark with a grayish-tan lining; the wide, light-colored tail is narrowly banded in black. Swainson's hawks also undergo a dark phase during which the entire body is dark brown. The wing linings and banded tail, however, remain unchanged. During flight the wings tilt slightly upward, whereas the wings of most predacious birds are perfectly horizontal.

HABITAT
Found in the plains and desert regions of Oregon, Nevada, Utah, Colorado, and New Mexico to 6,000 feet in elevation. The nest is a stick platform lined with grass or soft leaves built in trees, large bushes, or cactus or yucca plants.

EGGS
2-4; pale blue spotted with brown.

VOICE
A high-pitched, drawn-out "kreeeee."

FOOD
Grasshoppers, crickets, small rodents, and reptiles.

ENEMIES
Man.

STATUS
During the early part of the 20th century, large gatherings of Swainson's hawks, sometimes numbering two or three thousand, were not uncommon. Today, though nowhere near that numerous, they are a common bird of prey in open country.

THINGS YOU SHOULD KNOW
Primarily insect eaters, Swainson's hawks are highly beneficial to farmers. According to studies by Dr. C. Hart Merriam, a single hawk will consume 6,000 grasshoppers per month.

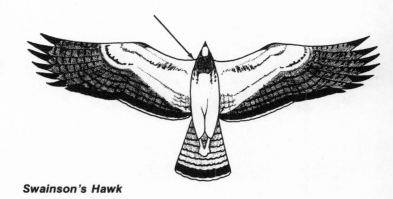

Swainson's Hawk

Swainson's Hawk (light phase)

Red-Tailed Hawk
(Buteo jamaicensis)

ALIAS
Chicken Hawk.

IDENTIFICATION
A large hawk, 2 feet long with a wingspread of 4½ feet. Adults undergo two coloration stages. During the light phase the chest, throat, and stomach are generally white, streaked with brown; the back is dark brown. During the dark phase the overall color is brownish-black. In both phases *the wide, rounded tail is reddish-brown* and is easily seen when the bird is in flight.

HABITAT
Found in all western states, Alaska, western Canada, and Mexico. Typical habitat is open country, scrub woodlands, or wide, rocky canyons. Red-tails, however, are adaptable and wide-ranging, and may be found almost anywhere. The nest is generally a platform of sticks or branches in a tall tree, cliff face, or yucca or cactus plant.

EGGS
2-3; white, splotched lightly with brown.

VOICE
In flight, a high-pitched "skeeeeer"; at close range, a croaking "guh-runk."

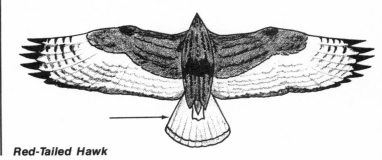

Red-Tailed Hawk

Red-Tailed Hawk (light phase)

Red-Tailed Hawk striking

FOOD

About 75 percent of a red-tail's diet consists of gophers, field mice, ground squirrels, rabbits, and insects. They also consume rattlesnakes and other reptiles as well as carrion.

ENEMIES

Red-tails are commonly attacked but not usually injured by crows, magpies, owls, other hawks, and even songbirds over territorial disputes. They do, however, suffer high losses from ranchers and farmers who, not realizing their great benefit in controlling rodents, shoot them off telephone poles.

STATUS

Common; probably the most often seen western bird of prey.

THINGS YOU SHOULD KNOW

Almost as unquenchable as a porcupine's passion for salt is a red-tail's taste for rattlesnake meat. Their legs are scaled, not feathered, for protection against snakebites, but they are not immune to hemotoxin, and may become the victim instead of the conqueror. Once a snake has been captured, its head is immediately torn away before the body is consumed.

Especially during mating season, red-tails are acrobatic technicians, often touching their mates in mid-air or dropping 2,000 feet in a single dive. Probably more than any other bird save the golden eagle, red-tails enjoy perching on telephone poles—a habit that has cost many their lives.

Turkey Vulture
(*Cathartes aura*)

ALIAS
Buzzard.

IDENTIFICATION
A very large, slender bird, 3 feet long with a wingspread of 6 feet. The basic body color is black, *with half-black, half-gray wings. The head is naked and generally red*; the tail is slender. While soaring, a vulture's wings tilt upward (dihedral inclination). They are masters of wheeling, circling flight.

HABITAT
Found from sea level to 10,000 feet in all western states, Canada, and Mexico, vultures have no typical habitat. They are most commonly sighted in flight, but they spend hours at a time roosting in tall trees or on a cliff face. Their favorite roosts can usually be identified by the "whitewash" (droppings) which stain the area below.

EGGS
2; dull white splotched with brown.

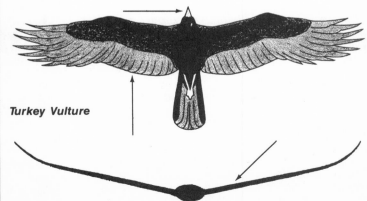

Turkey Vulture

Turkey Vulture (dihedral wing inclination)

Turkey Vulture

Turkey Vulture

VOICE
Silent except for a low, angry hiss when excited.

FOOD
Perhaps the turkey vulture's only benefit to man is its diet. Unable to capture and kill prey because of its foot construction, the vulture lives on carrion, able to strip large animals to the bone in a few days, and smaller ones in a few hours. Ridding the landscape of rotting animals is a major aid in disease control, and one at which vultures are truly adept. In most cases a vulture must wait for a dead animal to putrefy before its beak can rip through the tough hide to the carcass.

ENEMIES
None; seldom disturbed, even by man.

STATUS
Common.

THINGS YOU SHOULD KNOW
Nature has equipped these big carrion eaters well. Their digestive tract kills any toxic strain of bacteria which might be encountered while feeding. Their head and neck are naked, so that bacteria or parasites that might attach themselves to the skin will be destroyed by sunlight. Their superior eyesight and sense of smell make them difficult to approach even at a feeding site.

Young vultures are fed by a process of regurgitation. The chicks, not really very particular, thrust their heads into the parent's throat, drinking, more than eating, their dinner.

Vultures are migratory birds, normally wintering in warmer areas, particularly Mexico. In northern Baja they perch by the thousands on top of cactus. As they spread their wings to dry, they look like a convention of gargoyles preparing for a feast.

Golden Eagle
(Aquila chrysaetos)

IDENTIFICATION

A very large bird of prey, 2½-3½ feet long with a wingspread approaching 8 feet. Adults are brownish-black with no other markings except for a set of yellowish hackles at the base of the neck on the back. Immature birds are dark with white splotches on the wings and tail. In flight, the wings are horizontal, with the tips angled slightly forward.

HABITAT

Found from sea level to 10,000 feet in all western states, Alaska, Canada, and Mexico. Typical habitat is rugged, rocky canyon country, open desert, or grassy plain. The nest is a large, well-constructed pile of sticks in a tall tree or on a cliff face. A favorite roost is atop a telephone pole.

EGGS

2; dull white or pinkish-white, speckled with brown.

Golden Eagle

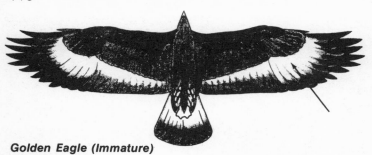

Golden Eagle (Immature)

Golden Eagle (Adult)

VOICE
A loud, rasping "kee-kee-kee."

FOOD
Golden eagles consume small mammals, birds, reptiles, jackrabbits, and carrion. They are probably one of the most efficient rodent controls in nature. They also take very young domestic livestock.

ENEMIES
Golden eagle populations have been reduced dramatically by the use of poisoned baits and traps, and by hunters who sometimes shoot them from airplanes with 12-gauge shotguns. The use of pesticides has caused some decline, especially in cultivated regions.

STATUS
Threatened.

THINGS YOU SHOULD KNOW
The following report by F. C. Willard was released in 1916: "The deer had been pounced upon by one or more eagles as it floundered in the deep snow, and its back was fearfully lacerated by the talons. After it had succumbed, the carcass was dragged downhill over one hundred yards until it lodged against a large boulder. Three eagles were feeding on it when first discovered by some prospectors."

It is this type of unbelievable hearsay that is primarily responsible for creating a villain of the golden eagle. Unfortunately, many ranchers believe such tales and mistakenly blame eagles for killing adult livestock. In all probability, the deer mentioned by Willard was killed by lions or starvation. It is highly doubtful that even several 15-pound birds would attack something as large as an adult whitetail buck, let alone be able to kill it. And to claim that they could drag the animal through deep snow is totally ridiculous.

The fact is, eagles are carrion eaters, often seen feeding on kills made by other predators. They cannot carry off children, horses, cattle, or deer. The well-known ornithologist E. S. Cameron states that the largest eagle could not carry anything heavier than 18 pounds at the extreme limit of its capacity.

Mating behavior between two golden eagles is an aerial circus. Their mid-air courtship includes rolls, steep dives, and headstands. Sometimes the birds actually touch in mid-flight.

Bald Eagle
(Haliaeetus leucocephalus)

IDENTIFICATION
A very large, soaring bird, 3½-4 feet long with a wingspread of 6-8 feet; next to the California condor, the bald eagle is America's largest bird of prey. The basic body color is grayish-black; *the head and tail are pure white and distinctly visible at a distance.* Immature birds are generally brownish-black; the body may be splotched with gray; the head and tail are sometimes gray but more often brownish.

HABITAT
Found in most of the western states, Canada, and Alaska. Primarily water birds, bald eagles usually reside near lakes, marshes, swamps, or large rivers. The most typical habitat is a steep river canyon. The nest is a large platform of sticks, grass, and mud, up to 20 feet deep and 10 feet in diameter, normally located in a tall tree.

Bald Eagle

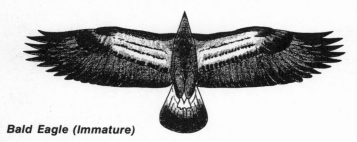

Bald Eagle (Immature)

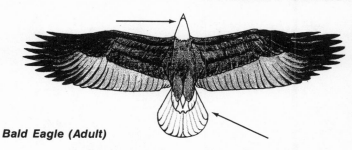

Bald Eagle (Adult)

EGGS
2; dull white or bluish-white.

VOICE
A "ki-ki-ki-ki."

FOOD
About 70 percent of a bald eagle's diet consists of fish, either captured fresh or stolen from other birds of prey. A bald eagle may also consume carrion, waterfowl, upland game, and rodents.

ENEMIES
Some scientists believe pesticides ingested by feeding adults are causing thin eggshells and prematurely hatching young, though this theory has not yet been proved. The eagle's habitat is also being destroyed as industrial or residential construction demolishes wetlands, nesting trees, and food sources. The largest number of deaths, however, results from shooting, usually by ranchers who mistakenly believe that bald eagles prey on livestock.

STATUS
Endangered; though protected under federal law, the bald eagle population continues to decline rapidly. Of the once numerous southern subspecies, only about 300 birds remain. The northern subspecies still numbers about 20,000 birds.

THINGS YOU SHOULD KNOW
Bald eagles have been America's national symbol since 1782, when over the objections of Benjamin Franklin, they were selected instead of the wild turkey. Strangely enough, they were not protected until the Bald Eagle Protection Act was passed in 1940. Protection came too late for many: 100,000 were killed in Alaska during the 35 years preceding, and hundreds of thousands more in the lower United States. Today it is unlawful to keep, kill, or otherwise harass a bald eagle without a special permit. No permits have been given other than for pure scientific research since 1969.

Most of the old wives' tales concerning bald eagles are false. They cannot, for example, carry off lambs, calves, dogs, or children. Only a very large bird can lift an object weighing more than 4 pounds. Most stories in which eagles have been accused of killing large animals stem from cases where they were seen feeding on already dead livestock.

Bald eagles have extraordinary vision and patience. They can spot movement 3 miles distant, and some have been known to sit motionless for nearly 4 hours. Their flight, too, is amazing. They can dive at speeds approaching 60 miles an hour and often migrate distances of 3,000 miles.

WATERFOWL

7/

NOTES ON WATERFOWL

Generally there are five varieties of waterfowl inhabiting western flyways—geese, surface-feeding ducks, diving ducks, stiff-tailed ducks, and mergansers. Only two, geese and surface feeders, are discussed to any extent in the following pages, but readers should be aware of the existence and differences in body design and behavior of the others.

Both Canada geese and snow geese can usually be recognized by their large size, distinctive voice, and characteristic coloration.

Surface-feeding ducks, commonly called puddle ducks, include mallards, pintails, gadwalls, widgeons, and most other "sporting" ducks. Large for the most part, they feed on or near the water's surface, seldom submerging themselves completely. They "dip" when they feed, turning themselves upside down in shallow water so that just their tail shows above the water. When leaving the water, puddle ducks leap straight into the air, combining initial wing movement for flight with a push from their webbed feet. On land, they can be distinguished by the position of their legs near the center of the body. The body itself is nearly parallel to the ground.

Puddle ducks feed by "dipping"–turning themselves upside down but seldom submerging completely.

Surface-feeding ducks, commonly known as puddle ducks, leave the water by flinging themselves straight into flight. Their feet are used only for the initial push.

Puddle ducks' legs are located near the center of the body. The body itself is nearly parallel to the ground.

Diving ducks, also called bay ducks, are generally smaller than puddle ducks and usually feed totally submerged, darting through the depths like needle-nosed fish. When leaving the water, they flop along the surface ("pattering"), using both their feet and wings to gain enough speed for takeoff. The legs are located near the tail, and on land, the body is at an angle with the head much higher than the tail.

Diving ducks can usually be identified on land by the rearward position of their legs and the steep angle of their bodies.

Diving ducks, or bay ducks patter across the water on takeoff, using their feet as much as their wings to gain momentum.

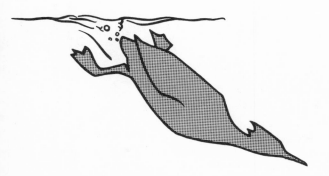

Diving ducks submerge completely when feeding. Most are excellent swimmers underwater.

Stiff-tailed ducks are small, well-rounded waterfowl with short, sharp tails that seem to erupt upward at a 45-degree angle. They feed both on and beneath the surface, and patter when leaving the water. Stifftails are seldom seen on land, since their short legs are nearly useless for walking.

Mergansers are large ducks with narrow, toothed bills. The head of most species has a crest of some type. They feed by diving and patter when leaving the water.

Most American waterfowl nest on the ground in the tundra regions of Canada, Alaska, Iceland, or Greenland during the summer. Their eggs are usually colored green, brown, or a combination of both, contrasting sharply with the eggs of most tree birds, which are usually white. The colored eggs of ground-nesting birds may represent an adaptation for survival, since the color acts as a camouflage to protect against predation.

In late summer, after the young waterfowl have gained sufficient size and strength to fly, huge flocks of ducks and geese migrate in arrowhead formation southward across the United States, using the stars as navigation aids. They usually arrive at their wintering grounds in the milder regions of the United States, Mexico, and South America by late fall or early winter. There they spend the cold months in relative comfort, returning to their nesting grounds in spring and early summer.

Mallard Duck
(Anas platyrhynchos)

ALIAS
Greenhead.

IDENTIFICATION
The largest "sporting" duck in western America, 24-36 inches long, weighing up to 3 pounds. *Males can be easily identified by their glossy green head and distinctive white neck ring.* The breast is deep brownish-red; the rump is black. The underparts and tail are white; the tail feathers curl slightly. Females are usually found near males. They are smaller and usually colored drab, mottled brown with light-colored tails. Both sexes have yellow bills and orange feet.

HABITAT
Probably the most common duck found on the western flyways, mallards may live around a lake, pond, grain field, or river, or even a tiny creek.

Mallard Duck (male)

VOICE
Males may make a soft, very identifiable "fwap-fwap-fwap"; females quack loudly.

FOOD
Grain, corn, mosses, aquatic plants.

ENEMIES
Mallards are the most sought-after sporting duck in America. Each year they make up at least one-third of the total North American duck kill. Natural predators are large, fast-flying hawks.

STATUS
Common.

THINGS YOU SHOULD KNOW
Easily domesticated, mallards grow to nearly twice their normal size when kept under ideal conditions by man. They are sold as food in many supermarkets.

Pintail Duck
(Anas acuta)

IDENTIFICATION
2 feet long, including the tail. The males are large, gray ducks with *long, needle-pointed tails*. The underparts are white; *the head is black with a curved vertical white stripe behind the eye*. The feet and bill are grayish-blue. The basic female coloration is mottled brown with gray feet and bill. The females do not have the slender, pointed tail; they are usually identified by close proximity to the males, both in flight and on the water.

HABITAT
Common on all western flyways. Typical habitat is river, lake, pond, marsh, or grain field.

VOICE
Males whistle distinctly; females quack.

Mallard Duck

Pintail Duck

Pintail Duck (female and male)

FOOD
Mosses, grain crops, aquatic vegetation.

ENEMIES
Among the top ten most hunted ducks in western America; natural predators are large hawks.

STATUS
Common.

THINGS YOU SHOULD KNOW
Throughout most of their migratory range, pintails are solitary ducks, not generally found in large flocks. The males, however, stick closely to their mates, and seldom is one seen without the other. Pintails are one of the earliest species to begin migration from their nesting areas in northern tundra, commonly arriving in the southern flyways during late August.

American Widgeon
(*Mareca americana*)

ALIAS
Baldpate.

IDENTIFICATION
A small duck, usually less than 2 feet long. The basic body color is grayish-brown with a bluish, mottled, black-tipped bill; the underparts are light gray or white. *Males have a conspicuous white crown and forehead with a shiny green eyepatch extending to the back of the head*. Widgeons are easily identified in flight by *the flashing white pattern of their wingbeats*, unique among puddle ducks.

HABITAT
Found in rivers, ponds, lakes, and marshes of the coastal and central western United States. They usually arrive from their summer nesting grounds about November.

VOICE
Males whistle; females quack loudly and explosively.

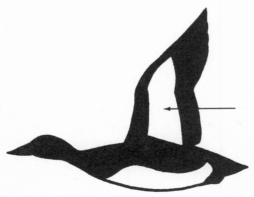

American Widgeon

American Widgeon (male)

American Widgeon (male)

FOOD

More than any other duck, widgeons prefer green food—mosses, succulent aquatic plants, and especially garden crops such as lettuce and spinach. They are seldom observed feeding on grain.

ENEMIES

Small, fast, and numerous, widgeons rank among the top five most hunted ducks in western flyways. Natural enemies are large, fast-flying birds of prey.

STATUS

Common.

THINGS YOU SHOULD KNOW

Of all American waterfowl, widgeons have probably adapted best to man's destruction of their wetland habitat. They seldom avoid humans, and sometimes even take up winter residence in such unlikely locations as ponds in golf courses or city parks. Extremely fond of garden crops—often man's replacement for their destroyed natural habitat—they feed heavily in cultivated fields.

Shoveler Duck
(*Spatula clypeata*)

ALIAS
Spoonbill Duck.

IDENTIFICATION
A small, slender duck, 17-21 inches long, *easily recognized by its long, heavy, spatula-shaped bill*. The male coloration is black and white, with white chest and shoulders and a metallic green head; during the spring courtship, the male's head may turn reddish. Females are brown with a spotted breast. Both sexes have orange legs and feet.

HABITAT
Found throughout the West, but mainly in the Rocky Mountain states. Typical habitat is marsh, pond, lake, river, or salt-water bay. Shovelers are early migrants, usually reaching their wintering grounds in peak numbers by November.

VOICE
Males "took-took"; females quack.

Shoveler Duck

Shoveler Duck

FOOD

Aquatic plants, insects, mosses. The shoveler's bill acts as a feeding aid, used either to skim insects and floating plants off the water's surface or to nip underwater plant stems.

ENEMIES

Large hawks; man is not a serious predator, since shovelers are not considered a sport duck.

STATUS

Common.

THINGS YOU SHOULD KNOW

Shovelers are perhaps the least wary of all waterfowl, usually approachable by humans to within 20 feet. Since they are primarily moss eaters and generally have fishy or muddy-tasting flesh, they are ignored by hunters.

Gadwall Duck
(Anas strepera)

IDENTIFICATION

A large duck, 2-2½ feet long, with *distinctive white patches on the hind edges of the wings, both below and above*. The patches are easily seen in flight. The males are scaly gray with *jet black rear ends*, light bellies, and yellow feet. The females are mottled brown with white underparts. The bills of both sexes are yellowish.

HABITAT

Found throughout western flyways. Typical habitat is marsh, lake, pond, or river. Gadwalls generally do not migrate far, shifting only a short distance south as the weather cools. Consequently, many nest in the northern United States instead of Alaska or Canada.

VOICE

Males whistle; the female's "quaaaaaaaack-qua-qua-qua-quack" is loud and drawn-out.

Gadwall Duck

FOOD

Insects, aquatic plants, and grain.

ENEMIES

Man, large birds of prey.

STATUS

Common.

THINGS YOU SHOULD KNOW

Gadwalls are primarily river ducks, often bypassing ponds and lakes for swifter streams. They are among the relatively few species of waterfowl that spend time during the summer feeding or resting at higher altitudes, commonly above 9,000 feet.

Gadwall Duck (male and female)

American Coot
(Fulica americana)

ALIAS
Mud Hen, Blue Peter.

IDENTIFICATION
A robust, dark gray water bird, 18-20 inches long; *the bill is white*. The head and neck often look nearly black; the feet are lobed, not webbed like a duck's. Coots are seldom found away from water. When swimming, they bob nervously with each foot stroke; fleeing from intruders, they patter across the water, using their feet as much as their wings.

HABITAT
Common and often permanent residents of marshes and lakes throughout the western United States. They are generally gregarious, congregating in flocks of 20-300.

VOICE
A harsh "kuk-kuk-kuk-kuk," usually voiced when fleeing.

American Coot

FOOD
All types of aquatic mosses, grasses, and insects.

ENEMIES
Natural predators are few, probably because coots have foul, oily-tasting flesh (they aren't called mud hens for nothing). Even birds of prey usually pass them by. They are sometimes shot by hunters who mistake them for ducks.

STATUS
Common.

THINGS YOU SHOULD KNOW
Because they have almost no natural predators, coots are found in great abundance in most wetland habitats, often competing heavily with ducks and geese for food. They are heartily disliked by sportsmen for this reason. However, coots fill an important role by keeping mosses and underwater vegetation at acceptable levels.

Snow Goose
(Chen hyperborea)

ALIAS
Blue Goose, Wawa.

IDENTIFICATION
A glossy, pure white goose, 2-3 feet long, with jet-black wing tips. The bill and feet are usually dusky-colored. Some snow geese undergo a dark color phase during which the body is bluish-gray. They fly in arrowhead formation.

Snow Goose

HABITAT
Found in all western flyways during fall and winter. Snow geese migrate southward early, usually reaching peak numbers by November. Typical habitat is wet, lowland marsh, corn or grain field, or rice paddy.

VOICE
Most commonly, a single loud honk as they pass overhead in flight; they also cackle and bark.

FOOD
Grain, corn, rice, aquatic plants.

ENEMIES
Snow geese are heavily hunted during the autumn and mid-winter shooting season. Human progress, however, has been their greatest enemy. Dams, pollutants, and industrial construction have destroyed nearly 50 million acres of wetland in the last 200 years. Natural predators are coyotes, badgers, and larger birds of prey.

STATUS
Common; an estimated 800,000 snow geese migrate southward each year.

THINGS YOU SHOULD KNOW
Snow geese are gregarious, apparently comfortable when they are bill to tailfeathers with several thousand of their kin. Groups of 30,000 are not an uncommon sight on abundant feeding grounds. They are excellent aviators, capable of non-stop trips from Hudson's Bay in Canada to the Gulf of Mexico. Their normal cruising altitude may be as high as 6,000 feet.

Snow Geese in flight

Snow Geese in typical habitat

Canada Goose
(Branta canadensis)

ALIAS
Honker, Bay Goose, Wild Goose, Mexican Goose, White-Cheeked Goose, Cackler Goose.

IDENTIFICATION
A large goose, 20-36 inches long with a wingspread of 5-7 feet. The body is gray with a light-colored breast and underparts. *The head and neck are totally black except for a large white cheek-patch (chin-strap) behind the eyes.* Canadas are the only geese to have such markings. The bill and feet are black; in flight, these big waterfowl form a long, sprawling V.

HABITAT
Found in all western flyways during the autumn and winter months. Typical habitat is lake, marsh, or cultivated field. Canada geese have been known to alight and feed in mountain tundra.

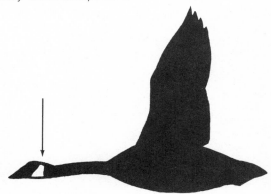

Canada Goose

VOICE

"Goose gabble," a constant babbling among individual geese or between flocks, is a well-known phenomenon to ornithologists and hunters. The birds use at least 10 vocalizations, the most common of which is an in-flight "uh-whonk," easily heard even though the flock may be out of sight. They also hiss and "wah-hummm." The Canada alert call is a loud "kwuk-grr."

FOOD

Grain plants of all types, especially corn; also cattails, clover, moss, and grass.

ENEMIES

A few Canada geese are taken by the very large predacious birds, but man and his devices are their only significant enemies. Several hundred thousand are killed each year by hunters. Mosquito control projects in which wetlands are drained have destroyed many thousands of acres of habitat. The lead shot used in shotgun shells may be eaten by geese, sometimes resulting in lead poisoning and eventual death.

Canada Geese in flight

Canada Geese in marsh habitat

STATUS

Like most species of American wildlife, geese have drastically declined in the past 200 years. The Canada goose's most trying period was 1850 to 1900, when the species was reduced to near extinction by unrestricted hunting and unorthodox decoying methods, most of which are illegal today. With the signing of the Migratory Bird Treaty, an agreement that gave limited protection to birds flying back and forth between Canada and Mexico, goose populations reestablished themselves. The world population of Canada geese today is estimated at 3 million.

THINGS YOU SHOULD KNOW

Of some 50 species of waterfowl, Canada geese are perhaps the best equipped for survival. Their superb hearing and eyesight is surpassed only by birds of prey. Their powerfully muscled bill and heavy wings are capable of putting most potential predators to flight. In addition, their instincts concerning danger are unique. For example, even in flight they usually avoid heavy grass or brush that could conceal an enemy.

Geese migrate in V formation for an excellent reason. Beginning with the point or lead bird (usually an adult female), each goose breaks the air for the next in line. Flying close behind and just off to one side for unobstructed vision, flock members take advantage of this frictionless air in much the same way as automobile racing drivers do. They are capable of speeds approaching 60 miles an hour, but their usual cruising speed is near 40. Flights have been observed by airplane pilots at 9,000 feet.

Probably the most original plan ever devised to hunt geese is reported by Joe Van Wormer in *The World of the Canada Goose*. Hunters would soak grain in whisky, and then scatter it in an empty field. Feeding geese would become too drunk to fly and could be picked up without firing a shot. Because of such practices and other heavy human predation, the average goose lives only three years.

Gulls

IDENTIFICATION
The 17 gull species found in the western states are similar in appearance and extremely difficult to tell apart at a distance or in flight. Immature gulls of almost all species, in fact, can usually be distinguished only by laboratory examination. However, some gulls can be identified by eye color and wing-tip variation. Listed below are the identification characteristics of the four most common.

Western Gull (Larus occidentalis). A large gull, 2-2½ feet long. The underparts are snowy white; the back and wings are dark. *The wing tips are black, but the trailing edge of the wing has a broad white band.* The legs and feet are pink; the bill is yellowish with a red spot near the end of the lower mandible; the eyes are light-colored. The voice is a soft "kak-kak-kak-kak" and a squeal.

Herring Gull (Larus argentatus). About 2 feet long; the body is white with gray wings tipped in black; the legs are pink; the bill is yellow with a red spot on the lower mandible; the eyes are brown.

California Gull (Larus californicus). Less than 2 feet long; the body is white; the wings and back are gray; the wings are tipped in black and white (mirrored); the legs are greenish-yellow; the bill is yellow with a red or black spot on the lower mandible; the eyes are black.

Ring-Billed Gull (Larus delowarensis). A small gull, 1½ feet long. The body is white; the back and wings are gray; the wings are tipped in black and white (mirrored). Ring-bills are easily recognized by the *narrow black band encircling the bill near the point.*

HABITAT
Found along the Pacific coast from Alaska to Mexico, and with the exception of the western gull, inland to the Dakotas. Typical habitat is harbor, beach, oceanside cliff, lake, cultivated field, or garbage dump. The ring-billed gull is probably the most common inland visitor.

FOOD
Omnivorous; they are scavengers consuming anything and everything handy, especially dead fish, clams, and mussels. Inland gulls eat large quantities of insects, worms, garbage, and garden crops.

ENEMIES
Human pollution; greatly affected by oil spills or sludged-over harbors. Natural predators are few.

STATUS
Common.

THINGS YOU SHOULD KNOW
The vultures of maritime environments, gulls are one of man's most beneficial friends and the primary reason that dead fish, garbage, and other waste products do not pollute coastal waters and recreation areas. The story is the same inland. In Utah, for instance, a monument erected in 1848 pays tribute to a "God sent" flight of California gulls that destroyed millions of crop-eating crickets about to consume a Mormon settlement's harvest.

Gulls have the unique habit of dropping edible mussels and clams from great heights to break them open. Like most sea birds, their wings are long and slender, naturally adapted for long periods of soaring. Their bills are heavy and slightly hooked, an adaptation which helps them tear up dead fish to eat.

Ring-Billed Gull

California Gull

Herring Gulls

Cormorants

IDENTIFICATION
The two most common of the 30 species known worldwide are described below.

Brandt's Cormorant (*Phalacrocorax penicillatus*). A large, vulture-like water bird, 30-36 inches long. The basic body color is brown or black with *a brownish band across the throat.* The bill is long, heavy, and slightly hooked at the end; the short, diamond-shaped tail usually drags the ground when the bird is motionless on land.

Double-Crested Cormorant (*Phalacrocorax auritus*). Similar to Brandt's cormorant except for *a yellowish throat.* Any cormorant sighted more than a few miles from the ocean is probably the double-crested species.

HABITAT
Rocky coastal beaches and harbors; inland lakes, large rivers, and swamps.

VOICE
Usually silent.

FOOD
Fish eaters; inland cormorants usually prefer rough fish—carp or suckers—which they catch under water. Ocean-dwelling species consume crustaceans as well as fish.

ENEMIES
Heavy aquatic pollution in certain areas has destroyed both habitat and food supplies. Large oil spills sometimes directly affect the birds, coating them with oil or sludge. They have no natural predators.

STATUS
Common.

THINGS YOU SHOULD KNOW
Cormorants are ancient birds which have existed relatively unchanged for nearly 50 million years. By nature they are aquatic, but they seldom leave sight of land. Excellent swimmers, they may dive to a depth of 100 feet, sometimes using their wings as swimming aids. In flight, cormorants often resemble geese.

In some parts of the world, cormorants are widely used in commercial fishing. Japanese and Chinese fishermen tether about a dozen birds to a boat by a long, flexible strap. Another strap is tied around each bird's throat to prevent it from swallowing. Then the cormorants are allowed to dive and fish. Once each bird has filled its throat, the fisherman draws it to the boat by the tether and removes the fish.

Mating cormorants generally present each other with a small piece of nesting material before switching places on the incubating eggs. The behavior is thought to reassure one parent that the other will not harm the nest if allowed to sit. Nesting cormorants should not be approached, since their incubation instincts are underdeveloped and both parents may permanently abandon the nest if frightened.

Brandt's Cormorant

Godwits

IDENTIFICATION
Two principal western species are described below.

Marbled Godwit (Limosa fedoa). A large, long-legged shore bird, 14-20 inches high. *The bill is extremely long and curves up.* The basic body color is mottled brown with slightly lighter underparts; the legs are grayish-black with knobby elbows; *the terminal half of the bill is generally black.* The voice is a "queep-queep" in flight and "terwhit-terwhit" on the ground.

Hudsonian Godwit (Limosa haemastica). Similar to the marbled godwit in appearance except for its slightly smaller size. The Hudsonian species is usually distinguished by a black tail and white rump. The voice is a soft "chip-chip."

HABITAT
Commonly observed along the Pacific coast from Oregon southward, and inland to the Dakotas and New Mexico. Typ-

Marbled Godwit

ical habitat is tide flat, sandy beach, or shallow pool or marsh.

FOOD
Insects, grubs, larvae, small mollusks.

ENEMIES
Natural predators are large hawks; a few are mistaken for game birds and killed by hunters. Perhaps their most serious enemy is pollution which destroys or poisons food supplies.

STATUS
Marbled godwits are common; the Hudsonian species is rare.

THINGS YOU SHOULD KNOW
The godwit uses its long, up-turned bill as a scoop and probe, gently pushing it through sand or water in search of small morsels.

Snowy Egret
(*Leucophoyx thula*)

IDENTIFICATION
A medium-sized, *pure white* wading bird, 20-24 inches high. *The bill and legs are long and black; the feet are yellow.* The head is generally crested with short plumes; the back is crested during mating season.

HABITAT
Found in western Canada, Alaska, and Mexico, and in all western states except Montana. Typical habitat is shallow marsh, river, or tide flat. The nest may be a reed or cattail platform in the water, or a platform of sticks in a bush. Egrets are often gregarious, sometimes feeding in colonies of up to 100.

EGGS
3-5; usually greenish-blue.

VOICE
A soft croak.

FOOD
Carnivorous; small fish and

Snowy Egret

mollusks, insects, aquatic reptiles.

ENEMIES
In some parts of the Americas, egrets are hunted for their plumes; natural predators are ground carnivores that may raid nests for young or eggs.

STATUS
Common.

THINGS YOU SHOULD KNOW
During the early part of the 20th century, hundreds of thousands of snowy egrets were killed each year for their plumes. The species was brought very close to total annihilation, but a dedicated effort on behalf of conservationists saved them from extinction. However, an active black market still exists for egret feathers.

Great Blue Heron
(Ardea herodias)

ALIAS
Fish Crane.

IDENTIFICATION
America's largest long-legged wading bird, 4 feet high with a wingspread of 6 feet. The body color is bluish-gray (it may look whitish in flight); the head is light-colored; the bill is long and heavy. There is a black stripe over the eye and a pair of plume-like feathers angling back from the head. In flight, herons can be distinguished from other large birds by their *U-shaped neck.*

HABITAT
Found throughout the western states, western Alaska, and western Canada. Typical habitat is tide flat, pond, river, marsh, or drainage canal. Herons are often sighted standing on one leg in shallow water or perched on a cliff or dead tree. Their nest is a stick platform usually constructed in a tree or on a rocky island. Except during mating season they are not gregarious.

EGGS
3-6; greenish-blue.

VOICE
A sharp croak.

FOOD
Small fish, snakes, frogs, salamanders, worms, crayfish, and occasionally small rodents.

ENEMIES
The adults have few natural predators, but the young, especially in ground nests, are eaten by any carnivore that may pass by. Herons are sometimes mistaken for geese or sandhill cranes and killed by sportsmen.

STATUS
Common.

THINGS YOU SHOULD KNOW
Herons use their long, ex-

Great Blue Heron

Great Blue Heron

Great Blue Heron in flight

tremely sharp bills to spear prey, whereas many other large wading birds grasp it between the two mandibles. In some areas herons have been accused of consuming large quantities of game fish, but 90 percent of their diet generally consists of carp, suckers, or chub.

All members of the heron family preen their feathers daily, using a waterproof, powder-like substance from a patch on their breast or rump. The powder, in reality, is frayed residue from "powder-down" feathers which are never shed and simply disintegrate from use. At one time heron plumes were so valuable that men were quite commonly killed fighting over them. The plumes were used for decorating garments, and efforts to obtain them nearly brought about the total destruction of heron populations. As many as 200,000 have been killed during a single year, just for their feathers.

Brown Pelican
(Pelecanus occidentalis)

ALIAS
Diving Pelican.

IDENTIFICATION
A large, cumbersome sea bird, 4-4½ feet long with a wingspread of 7-8 feet. The body is grayish-brown with a light-colored head and underparts; the bill is long, pouched, and slightly hooked at the terminal end; the head is streaked with red. A pelican's flight pattern consists of 300-foot glides with a few powerful flaps in between. Except when feeding, pelicans generally fly low, their wing tips sometimes touching the water to take advantage of the frictionless air near the waves.

HABITAT
Found along the central California coast and south to Mexico and South America. Large colonies reside in the Gulf of Cortez, primarily on the Baja Peninsula. Typical habitat is rugged, rocky shoreline, mangrove swamp, or uninhabited harbor.

VOICE
A harsh croak.

FOOD
Fish eaters; sardines or other small school fish are preferred. The brown pelican's feeding behavior is an amazing combination of timing and excellent vision. When prey is sighted, a pelican may plunge like a bullet from a height of 100 feet, folding its wings and extending its bill at the instant of impact to cleave the water with barely a splash. Beneath the surface, the bill balloons open and handily scoops in the prey. A few seconds later, the bird pops to the surface, lifts its bill to drain the water, and then swallows its catch.

ENEMIES
Pollution and pesticides. Once numbering in the hundreds of thousands, pelican populations have been dramatically reduced by the indirect ingestion of DDT and other pesticides used for agricultural pest control. DDT is a collective poison, passed from field to ocean and finally to pelicans through the ingestion of fish. Although it

A swooping Brown Pelican

rarely kills adult birds outright, DDT causes thin eggshells, which break before the young are ready to be hatched.

STATUS
Endangered. The total population in the United States probably does not exceed 14,000. The Mexican population is stable, however.

THINGS YOU SHOULD KNOW
The largest brown pelican concentrations are found along the Sea of Cortez in Baja, Mexico, between Mulege and Loreto. Here, where uninhabited coastal cliffs meet the sea, pelicans feed constantly and can be observed with little effort. However, observers should know that the penalty for killing, harming, or harassing a brown pelican is a $10,000 fine and/or one year in prison.

Brown Pelican

Sandhill Crane
(Grus canadensis)

ALIAS
Prairie Goose.

IDENTIFICATION
A long-legged, knobby-kneed land bird, 3½-4 feet high with a wingspread of 5-7 feet. The body color is slate gray; *the head has a rusty-colored crown*; the bill is 5-6 inches long. The short, tufted tail is often splotched with brown. In flight, a crane's long neck is extended forward and its legs are extended back. The flight formation is usually a wide V. Sandhills are gregarious and often observed in flocks of 20-300.

HABITAT
Found in all western flyways, usually in the same general area as geese. Occasionally flocks alight in high mountain meadows to feed.

VOICE
A loud, harsh "garoooa-a-a" while on the ground; in flight, an "onk-onk," sounding much

Sandhill Crane

Sandhill Crane

like the creaking of a rusty hinge.

ENEMIES
Few natural predators take these large cranes because of their inborn caution and highly developed senses. Their sight especially is extraordinary. Iced-over feeding grounds result in starvation for several thousand every year; some states still have tightly restricted hunting seasons.

STATUS
Uncommon. At one time, with less than 4,000 remaining in the wild, sandhill cranes were in grave danger of extinction. At the urging of wildlife organizations, most states added a "no-kill" restriction to their game laws, and sandhills slowly but steadily increased in number to their present level of about 20,000.

THINGS YOU SHOULD KNOW
Sandhill courting behavior takes place in the spring and includes a unique display of "dancing"—a series of 15-foot leaps combined with a flut-

Sandhill Crane in flight

Sandhill Cranes

tering exhibition of wing flapping. The red patch or bald spot on a crane's head brightens significantly during the mating season.

Excellent aviators, these big birds are capable of migrating 3,000 miles and flying at altitudes of 14,000 feet. On the ground they move rapidly, able to outdistance human beings with ease.

In 1975 a small flock of sandhills became foster parents in an attempt to save an endangered relative, the whooping crane. Whooping crane eggs removed from nests in Canada were placed beneath adult sandhills nesting in Idaho. The eggs hatched normally, and the chicks readily accepted their foster parents. Biologists hope the adopted chicks will breed with whooping crane mates, thereby increasing the dwindling population (in 1976 only 57 whooping cranes remained).

8/

GROUND AND UPLAND BIRDS

Roadrunner
(Geococcyx californianus)

ALIAS
Chaparral, Ground Cuckoo.

IDENTIFICATION
A slender, long-tailed ground bird, 1½-2 feet long, usually colored brown or gray and splotched with white. The underparts are light-colored; the bill is long and heavy. When excited, roadrunners erect a set of gaudy crest feathers. Their short, stubby wings do not permit long flight, but they are extremely fast runners. Their feet are zygodactyl, with two toes forward and two toes back (see Glossary of Animal Tracks).

HABITAT
Found in California, the southwestern states, and east to Louisiana. Typical habitat is open desert, creosote flat, or piñon-juniper scrub. Only occasionally are roadrunners seen above 6,000 feet. They nest on the ground or in low bushes.

Roadrunner

Roadrunner

EGGS
4-7; white.

VOICE
A quiet "coo-coo."

FOOD
Lizards, small mammals, insects, and sometimes carrion. Roadrunners also attack and consume small reptiles, including rattlesnakes.

ENEMIES
Fast and cautious, roadrunners have few natural predators. They are protected in most states.

STATUS
Common.

THINGS YOU SHOULD KNOW
When frightened or in a hurry, roadrunners are capable of running up to 30 miles an hour, negotiating a zig-zag obstacle course through heavy brush that few predators could hope to follow. When really pressed, they can fly, but usually not more than a few hundred yards. Their strategy against poisonous snakes depends on this same flashing speed for success. It is a matter of dodge and peck, dodge and peck, until the snake is exhausted and the bird can deliver a killing blow with its razor-sharp bill.

Common Crow
(Corvus brachyrhynchos)

ALIAS
Western Crow.

IDENTIFICATION
17-20 inches long; the basic body color is dead black, tending to deep purple or violet in bright sunlight. The bill and feet are black. *Crows are much smaller than ravens.*

HABITAT
Crows are found throughout the western United States, but more common west of the

Common Crow. About the size of a large pigeon.

Common Crow

Rocky Mountains. Their range encompasses all types of terrain from sea level to 10,000 feet. The nest is a crude but carefully lined platform of sticks, usually constructed in a tree. Crows are gregarious, often observed in flocks numbering into the hundreds.

EGGS
4-6; greenish.

VOICE
A harsh "caw-caw."

FOOD
Omnivorous; carrion, garbage, small rodents, young birds, reptiles, and vegetable matter, especially garden and farm crops.

ENEMIES
No serious natural predators; in some states they are agricultural pests and are hunted and trapped by humans.

STATUS
Common.

THINGS YOU SHOULD KNOW
Some observers suggest that crows and ravens are wary of man's approach because of their conspicuous black coloration. Birds with camouflaged feathers are generally less nervous than those with easily seen plumage. The birds themselves seem to know they make an easy target.

Crows are intelligent and make excellent pets. They can easily be taught to laugh and imitate human voices. However, baby crows eat at least half their weight each day and usually more as their age increases. Many young birds starve to death in captivity because their well-meaning owners do not feed them enough.

Common Raven
(Corvis corax)

ALIAS
American Raven.

IDENTIFICATION
A large, glossy black bird, 21-27 inches long; the bill is large and heavy; the nostrils are covered by bristly feathers called filoplumes. *Ravens usually display a large tuft of feathers at their throat* (goiter). *Their flight pattern is flap-soar-flap.*

Common Raven. Larger than the crow. The tuft of throat feathers (goiter) is usually visible at a distance.

HABITAT
Found at altitudes of 4,000-12,000 feet in all western states, Canada, Alaska, and Mexico, in all types of terrain. A raven's nest is a large, crude stick platform on a cliff face, in a tall tree, or on the ground.

EGGS
5-7; greenish with brown spots.

VOICE
A loud, hoarse croak.

FOOD
Omnivorous; carrion, garbage, small mammals, young birds, vegetable matter.

ENEMIES
Considered a pest throughout much of their range, ravens are commonly shot by humans. They have no natural predators.

STATUS
Common.

THINGS YOU SHOULD KNOW
Ravens have a strong territorial instinct, viciously attacking owls, hawks, and even eagles who intrude on their domain.

Sportsmen sometimes use this trait to their advantage by baiting a clearing with tethered owl decoys and then shooting the ravens from blinds as they attempt to drive the intruders away.

Common Raven

Mourning Dove
(Zenaidura macrourua)

ALIAS
Turtle Dove.

IDENTIFICATION
A fast-flying, grayish-brown bird, usually less than 12 inches long. *The tail is pointed and spotted with white*; the head is round and bullet-shaped; the feathers are smooth and silky; the bill and feet are black.

Mourning Dove

Mourning Dove

HABITAT
Found throughout the western states, Canada, and Mexico from sea level to 13,000 feet, usually in the vicinity of water. Typical habitat may be cultivated field, open meadow, or desert. Doves are generally active in early morning or late evening. The nest is a small, grass-lined platform of sticks in a tree or bush, or a platform of grass on the ground.

EGGS
2; white.

VOICE
A series of three soft coos, the first of which is almost inaudible.

FOOD
Weed seeds, especially sunflower seeds, and grain crops.

ENEMIES
Doves are occasionally taken by very fast birds of prey and ground carnivores, and they are heavily hunted by sportsmen throughout the United States. Their ground nests are often destroyed by tractors, foraging livestock, and reptiles.

STATUS
Common.

THINGS YOU SHOULD KNOW
Of all upland birds, mourning doves are perhaps the least susceptible to drought, flood, and other adverse weather conditions, mainly because they can fly great distances quickly (their top speed is 40 miles per hour) to escape such quirks of nature. They are also extremely prolific and may nest several times a year.

Young doves are fed by a process of regurgitation in which they take a partially digested substance called "pigeon's milk" from the parent's throat.

Mourning doves use their wings as tools for knocking seeds from plants like sunflowers and poppies.

White-Winged Dove
(Zenaida asiatica)

IDENTIFICATION
A grayish-brown bird, slightly larger than a mourning dove, with a *rounded, white-tipped tail*; the only American dove with large white wing patches. In flight white-winged doves can be distinguished by the flashing white pattern of their wing-beats.

HABITAT
Found throughout the western United States but more commonly in California, Nevada,

White-Winged Dove

Arizona, and Texas. Typical habitat is open prairie, desert, or mesquite forest. However, the doves often feed in cultivated fields. The nest is a small, slightly hollowed twig platform in a tree, barely sufficient to contain the eggs.

EGGS
2; light brown or white.

VOICE
A harsh "coo-oo-ooh."

FOOD
Weed seeds, grains, mesquite beans, wild grass seeds.

ENEMIES
In most states there is no distinction between hunting seasons for the mourning and white-winged doves. Natural predators are birds of prey and small land carnivores.

STATUS
Unusual.

THINGS YOU SHOULD KNOW
White-winged and mourning doves are perhaps the best natural weed destroyers on

earth. A single dove may consume 100 pounds of weed seeds each year.

White-wing nestlings are fed with "pigeon's milk," a regurgitated substance from the parent's stomach.

White-Winged Dove

Quail

IDENTIFICATION

Quail are plump, pigeon-sized ground birds, usually contrastingly colored with some type of crest or top-knot easily visible. Discussed below are the five most common western species.

Gambel's Quail (*Lophortyx gambelii*). Alias Redhead Quail. 12 inches high; the males are gray with buff underparts and reddish-brown sides and wings, streaked heavily with white. *The crest is a short black plume* thrusting upward and forward from a reddish crown. *The face is masked with a circle of black above and below the bill.* The females have a shorter brown plume with no facial mask. Gambel's quail are found from sea level to 6,500 feet in California, Arizona, Nevada, Utah, Colorado, New Mexico, and Texas. Typical habitat is brushy terrain near water. *They roost in trees or high bushes.* The voice is a "quaieeeeer," with the accent on the last syllable, or a "chu-kee-ta." When threat-ened, they utter a throaty "pweep" or a "whup-whup-pweep." Eggs: 10-15, white splotched with brown.

California Quail (*Lophortyx californicus*). 11 inches long; very similar to Gambel's quail except for a scaly underbelly. Found in California, Oregon, Washington, Idaho, Utah, and Nevada. Habitat and voice are identical to that of Gambel's. Eggs: 10-20, white spotted with brown.

Scaled Quail (*Callipepla squamata*). Alias Blue Quail, Cactus Quail, Desert Quail, Cotton-Topped Quail. 10 inches high; both sexes alike. The body color is light gray with distinctive, scale-like feathers on the chest and back. *The crest is a 1-inch gray and white triangle of feathers angling back from the bill.* Excellent runners, scaled quail are seldom coaxed into flight. Found in arid desert regions and sagebrush flats of New Mexico, Arizona, Texas, Colorado, and Oklahoma below 7,000 feet; *they are the quail most commonly observed far from water.* The voice is a distinctive "back-off," with the accent on the second syllable. Eggs: 10-15, light brown with white speckles.

Bobwhite Quail (*Colinus virginianus*). 8-10 inches high; *distinguished from other quail by their very small crest.* The basic body color is dark brown, striped with tan bars. The underparts are white; there is a distinctive white throat patch beneath the bill. Found in lowland areas, cultivated fields, fence rows, and thickly wooded areas of Washington, Oregon, Wyoming, eastern Colorado, eastern New Mexico, and Texas. The voice is an unmistakable "bob-white." Eggs: 10-20, usually dull white.

Gambel's and California Quail

Scaled Quail

Bobwhite Quail

Gambel's Quail (male and female)

Scaled Quail

Bobwhite Quail (male)

Mountain Quail *(Oreortyx picta).* Alias Painted Quail, Plumed Quail. 11 inches high; *the crest is a long, slender black plume, thrusting straight up from the head.* The body color is brown with a gray head and chest, and a reddish throat; the undersides are barred with brown and white. Found on temperate mountain slopes or in heavily brushed forests in Washington, Oregon, California, and Nevada. The voice is a whistle, a harsh "krawk," or a "took-took-took." Eggs: 6-15, reddish-brown.

Mountain Quail

FOOD
Mainly weed seeds, grain, and insects.

ENEMIES
Quail are pursued by every meat-eating mammal, predacious bird, and reptile in their range. They suffer unusually heavy losses from domestic cats, who often stalk the birds in their roosts. Desert or lowland species are constantly beset by flash floods, droughts, and brush fires, which usually occur in the spring when the chicks are young and vulnerable. Mountain-dwelling varieties may die of starvation during heavy snowfalls. Man is an enemy in the fall, killing millions during the legal hunting season.

STATUS
The masked bobwhite, an Arizona subspecies of bobwhite, is an Endangered Species. All others are prolific breeders and common throughout their range.

THINGS YOU SHOULD KNOW
Quail generally have an efficient sentry system, always on the alert for intruders while the rest of the covey is feeding. These silent sentinels usually lead enemies away from the congregation with a realistic broken-wing act. Most quail roost in tightly packed groups, tail to tail, with their heads pointed outward—a behavior that allows an all-night sentry system as well as conserving heat.

Most quail prefer to run or hide instead of flying when intruded on. Of all the species, Gambel's are the most cunning, able to disappear mysteriously on the ground or flutter into rapid, startling flight if danger gets too near. They are extremely practiced at frustrating hunters, using every bit of cover available, even if they must resort to scrambling down a prairie dog hole or hiding in a packrat's nest. Bobwhites, on the other hand, often avoid pursuers by hiding in grass or brush until literally stepped on, then exploding into erratic flight. Scaled quail are swift runners, easily able to outdistance a human being, even on level ground.

Chukar *(Alectoris graeca)*

IDENTIFICATION
A plump, chicken-sized bird, 12-14 inches high; the body color is gray, with distinct black and white vertical stripes on the sides. The face and throat are white, surrounded by a necklace of black; the bill and legs are reddish.

HABITAT
Chukars are an exotic species, native to Turkey and India but introduced into most western mountainous areas below 8,000 feet with varying degrees of success. They have also

Chukar

been brought into desert areas in the Southwest. A chukar's main requirement for survival is a nearby water supply and adequate feeding grounds, primarily grassy slopes. Chukars usually roost tail to tail on large rocks or the ground. Their nest is a ground depression lined with grass or feathers.

EGGS
7-15; yellowish or brown, speckled with purple.

FOOD
Cheat grass seeds, weed seeds, insects, wild berries.

VOICE
"Chuk-chuk," "cha-ker," and "wheet-up." The alert call is a sharp "kerrrr."

ENEMIES
The mortality rate of chukars due to harsh winter weather is 50-80 percent of the entire species. Great horned owls, coyotes, bobcats, and foxes take many. Man is not a serious predator, though hunting seasons exist in some states.

Chukar

STATUS
Unusual; chukars have not done well in most parts of their range, primarily because of cold winters. They have perhaps been most successful in the Southwest, where winters are mild.

THINGS YOU SHOULD KNOW
First introduced into America in 1893, chukars were stocked in 38 states. For some unknown reason, however, they survived only in the West. Chukars tend to migrate (unlike most ground-dwelling birds) up to 50 miles a year in search of food and water. They can go a week without drinking if necessary.

Grouse

IDENTIFICATION
Ten species and several sub-species of grouse and ptarmigan exist in the western United States; most exhibit similar characteristics and have overlapping ranges. They are all plump, chunky birds, acquiring camouflaged feathers early in life as a protection against predators. Discussed below are the four species most likely to be encountered.

Spruce Grouse (*Canachites canadensis*). Alias Franklin's Grouse. A chicken-sized bird, 1½ feet high, colored brownish-gray or black. The males usually have a black chest, and the females are speckled. The tail is dark and rounded with bold white markings on top. Found in Alaska, Canada, and the northern fringes of the American Rocky Mountains. The nest is a depression in the ground lined with grasses or feathers, usually near a log or stump. Eggs: 8-15; brown with speckles.

Franklin's Grouse

Sharp-Tailed Grouse (Pedioecetes phasianellus). 1½ feet long; the body color is mottled brown with light-colored underparts. *The tail is short, sharp, and lightly banded with brown*; the head has a slight crest. Found in prairie regions or lowland forests of eastern Oregon, Idaho, Utah, New Mexico, and Canada. The voice is a low, soft coo; the nest is a depression in the ground lined with grass or plant fibers. Eggs: 10-15; olive-colored.

Blue Grouse (Dendragapus obscurus). Alias Dusky Grouse, Sooty Grouse. Western America's most common grouse; a bluish-gray bird, 2 feet long, with a long, black-tipped tail. The legs and underparts are white; the head has a small crest. Found usually above 7,000 feet in Alaska, Canada, and most of the western states. Typical habitat is heavy forest or brushy meadow. The voice is a soft "hut-hut" or a series of hoots. The nest is a depression in the ground lined with pine needles at the base of a rock, stump, or tree. Eggs: 5-15; pinkish-tan spotted with brown.

White-Tailed Ptarmigan (Lagopus leucurus). Alias Snow Grouse. *A small, white-tailed bird, usually less than 1 foot long.* The bill, eyes, and feet are black; in summer, the coloration is mottled brown and white with light-colored underparts and fully feathered legs. *In winter, the color is pure white.* Found in the Rocky Mountains south to New Mexico. Typical habitat is alpine country or tundra; even during harsh winters, ptarmigan survive in high altitudes by burrowing themselves into a snowbank for warmth and shelter. The voice is a "kuk-kuk-kuk"; the nest is a shallow, rocky depression in the ground. Eggs: 5-10; brown.

FOOD

Most grouse survive on acorns, insects, wild berries, and succulent plants. The mountain-dwelling species eat spruce and fir needles in the winter when little else is available.

White-Tailed Ptarmigan

ENEMIES

Throughout their range, grouse are preyed on by every land carnivore and meat-eating bird able to catch them. Most species are hunted by man during a short autumn season. Unlike most large ground-dwelling birds, grouse are not seriously affected by harsh winters.

STATUS

Common.

THINGS YOU SHOULD KNOW

Most grouse are robust animals, fully equipped for survival in rugged mountain or prairie regions. They are born precocious—fully feathered with their eyes open—an adaptation that protects the young from predation. Their plumage is thick and heavy, and their feet are usually feathered to act as snowshoes in deep snow. Although classified as ground birds, during extremely harsh winters grouse may spend much of their time in trees, feeding on buds or needles. (Ptarmigan, which burrow into snowbanks, are an exception.)

Wild Turkey
(*Meleagris gallopavo*)

ALIAS

Gobbler.

IDENTIFICATION

A slender, more muscular version of a domestic turkey, 3-4 feet high, weighing 10-20 pounds. The basic color is camouflaged bronze-gray; the head is reddish-blue and naked; the tail is broad and tipped in white; the legs are long and naked. Males have conspicuous breast appendages called beards, 6-7 inches long. Both sexes exhibit brightly colored wattles on the head and chin. During mating season, wattles on the male generally turn blood red.

HABITAT

Traditionally found only in Colorado, New Mexico, Arizona, and western Texas, wild turkeys are now common in most of the western states and the Dakotas as a result of transplanting. Typical habitat is brushy, uninhabited pine forest or rugged scrub woodland above 6,000 feet. During daylight hours, turkeys usually remain in a high vantage point on or near a mountain peak or high ridge, shifting at dawn and dusk to lower slopes or valleys to forage. Gregarious, turkeys travel in flocks of 10-20. The nest is a depression in the ground beneath a bush or in high grass.

EGGS

10-15; light brown.

VOICE

One of the most intriguing forest calls is the short, loud "gobbleobbleobble" of active turkeys. Usually voiced in the early morning or late evening, it can be heard as far as a mile.

FOOD

Wild nuts, seeds, succulent plants, rose hips, wild grapes, and occasionally grass.

ENEMIES

Natural predators are coyotes, bobcats, lions, and foxes. Turkeys are hunted during short seasons in fall and spring. However, the destruction of their habitat by forest fire is probably their greatest enemy.

STATUS

Once common, even abundant, in their four-state ancestral range, turkeys received no protection during the late 19th and early 20th centuries. By 1920 they were facing extinction. Only with strict regulations and transplants of wild Texas turkeys were the birds reestablished. Today their population is slowly but steadily increasing.

THINGS YOU SHOULD KNOW

The turkey was probably the first animal in the Americas to be domesticated, tamed first by the Aztecs of Mexico and later by southwestern Pueblo Indians. Turkeys were used for decorative feathers and bones, and only occasionally for food.

Turkeys exhibit exceptional senses of sight and hearing. They are capable of flying at 55 miles per hour and running at 18. They were almost, but not quite, selected as America's national symbol. "I wish the bald eagle had not been chosen," said Benjamin Franklin, "as the Representative of our Country; he is a bird of bad moral Character; like those among Men who live by sharping and Robbing, he is generally poor, and often very lousy. The Turkey is a much more respectable Bird, and withal a true original Native of America."

Wild Turkey

9/ NONVENEMOUS SNAKES

Common Garter Snake
(Thamnophis sirtails)

IDENTIFICATION
A small, slender reptile seldom reaching 3 feet in length. *Most garter snakes have three light-colored stripes down their back and sides, with dark checks in between.* The head is generally colored black or olive and is wider than the neck; the lower jaw is tiger-striped; the tail is long and slender, striped to the tip.

HABITAT
Excellent swimmers (some subspecies, in fact, are totally aquatic), garter snakes are normally found in the vicinity of water, whether pond, marsh, river, or lake. They are probably the most common American reptile seen by humans.

FOOD
Carnivorous; small fish, frogs, snails, earthworms, tadpoles, salamanders, and young birds. Garter snakes have voracious appetites and they often attack food far too large for them to swallow.

Common Garter Snake

ENEMIES
All meat-eating land carnivores and predacious birds, as well as fish and other reptiles.

STATUS
Common.

THINGS YOU SHOULD KNOW
The female emits a strong perfume that both attracts and excites males during the mating season. She also has the unique capacity to store sperm after copulation in order to fertilize eggs she will produce much later.

Gopher Snake
(Pituophis melanoleucus)

ALIAS
Bull Snake.

IDENTIFICATION
A large, heavy-bodied snake attaining a length of 8 feet; the average, however, is 3-5 feet. The basic body coloration is cream or yellowish with dark, diamond-shaped blotches along the back. There also may be several rows of smaller dark patches along the sides. The head is slightly triangular and may have a dark horizontal line in front of the eyes. The gopher snake's defensive behavior is distinctive: it gives a very loud, raspy hiss while shaking and coiling its tail, much like a rattlesnake.

HABITAT
Found in all western states, Canada, and Mexico, from sea level to 10,000 feet. Exceptional hunters, gopher snakes prefer cultivated land, rocky areas, or brushy deserts that support large rodent populations. Active at dusk or during the night, they are seldom observed in the heat of the day.

FOOD
Mice, rats, ground squirrels, birds, and occasionally eggs, even though gopher snakes are not good climbers.

ENEMIES
Because of their unusual size and rattlesnake-like coloration, gopher snakes are quite often mistaken for rattlers and killed by humans. Farmers and ranchers fail to realize that this large serpent is one of nature's most efficient rodent controls. Natural predators are primarily hawks and eagles.

STATUS
Common.

THINGS YOU SHOULD KNOW
Gopher snakes are nonvenomous, but the bite of a large one may be painful. Once tamed, however, they make excellent pets.

According to herpetologists Charles Shaw and Sheldon Campbell, gopher snakes received their name because they use their coils to clear away dirt from gopher mounds, and then pursue the digging animals into their burrows.

Gopher Snake

Kingsnake
(Lampropeltis getulus)

IDENTIFICATION
A gaudily colored reptile reaching a length of 5 feet. The basic *coloration is highly variable*, but the general pattern is yellow or cream with distinct wide black or brown stripes across or down the back and sides. The head is rounded and the same width as the body. Two subspecies, the California Mountain and Sonora Mountain kingsnakes, are usually red and black with yellow bands across the back.

HABITAT
Found below 7,000 feet in Oregon, California, Nevada, Utah, Arizona, New Mexico, Texas, and Mexico, in all types of terrain but usually in the vicinity of water.

FOOD
Immune to the hemotoxin of rattlesnakes, kingsnakes kill and eat them whenever their paths cross. A kingsnake's diet includes all other types of snakes, rodents, birds, and lizards as well.

ENEMIES
Other kingsnakes, predacious birds, automobiles, and man.

STATUS
Common.

THINGS YOU SHOULD KNOW
Besides man, kingsnakes are probably the only living creatures that rattlesnakes truly fear. When the two meet, the rattler usually backs off, head and tail close to the ground so that the kingsnake can find no purchase for its coils. Strangely enough, however, threatened kingsnakes rattle their tails, coil, and strike, just as rattlers do. They also emit a smelly musk, used for defensive purposes and as sex stimulation to potential mates. Rattlesnakes are sometimes able to sense this musk and avoid a kingsnake's territory.

Kingsnake

Western Hognose Snake
(*Heterodon nasicus*)

ALIAS
Flat-Headed Adder, Hissing Adder, Puff Adder, Sand Viper.

IDENTIFICATION
A small, thick-bodied reptile, not more than a yard long. Its coloration is generally yellow or pale brown with dime-sized black or brown blotches down the back and sides. *The snout is flat and turned up, resembling the prow of a barge.*

HABITAT
Found from eastern Montana, south to Arizona. Typical habitat is sandy or rocky soil, blanketed with brush or scrub timber.

FOOD
Frogs, lizards, small mammals, and toads. Although most toads secrete a toxic substance, repellent and even deadly to some animals, special glands in the body of a hognose snake offset these secretions.

ENEMIES
Birds of prey, meat-eating mammals, and automobiles.

STATUS
Common.

THINGS YOU SHOULD KNOW
Hognose snakes are harmless, interesting, and if handled correctly, make excellent pets. However, at least one case has been reported in which a human was bitten and suffered pain and swelling in the bite area for a few hours. Though not considered venomous, the hognose is thought to be a primitive example of venomous reptile development, since studies indicate that it has enlarged parotid glands—the glands that in poisonous snakes produce venom.

Elongated anterior ribs enable a hognose to flatten his neck and head into a sinister hood. Combined with a threatening pose and loud hiss, this seldom fails to discourage attackers. However, if the predator is persistent, the hognose may go

Western Hognose Snake

into convulsions, snapping open his mouth and wiggling spastically. As a last resort, he may roll onto his back and play dead, becoming as limp as overcooked spaghetti. The only flaw in the act is that if turned over, he will promptly roll onto his back again.

RATTLESNAKES

NOTES ON RATTLESNAKES

Since their first encounter with man centuries ago, rattlesnakes have been surrounded by a cloak of mystery and mythology. As a result, most people automatically react to these beneficial reptiles with horror. True, except for the Gila monster and a small, extremely rare desert serpent called the Sonoran coral snake, rattlesnakes are the only small vertebrates in western America capable of killing an adult human with a single bite. But rattlers are neither mysterious nor superanimals, and most of the old wives' tales surrounding them are totally false.

Like most other carnivores, rattlesnakes are equipped with food-gathering devices that double as defense mechanisms. Their hemotoxic venom —used primarily to disable prey—is injected into a victim by a pair of hollow, folding fangs located in the upper jaw. It can be fatal to humans only if injected in this way. Swallowed venom is harmless, unless an ulcer is present which would allow it to reach the bloodstream. And contrary to popular belief, a snake's rattles do not carry or emit toxin of any type. The rattles are made of a skin-like substance, much like the horns of mammals, and do not come into contact with the glands containing venom.

Several times annually rattlesnakes shed their skin. Following each shed, a new button is added to the rattles. Consequently, the number of rattles on a snake's tail is no indication of its age. During the shed a rattlesnake's vision is slightly reduced, giving rise to the myth that rattlesnakes are blind and will strike at anything. Not so. A rattlesnake's strike is directed by heat and sense organs found in the tongue and head which are unaffected by the skin loss; eyes are not necessary for a direct hit. Nor do rattlesnakes have to be coiled to strike. They can strike from any position and in any direction at about the speed of a good boxer's right jab. The strike is usually one-third to one-half their length.

Rattlesnakes are probably more common in early spring (not in July as some would have us believe) when they abandon hibernation in search of food. Depending on their size and the available food supplies, they generally feed once a week, usually on mice or rats. Extremely susceptible to heat and cold, and unable to control their own body temperature, they are most active at dusk and during the early night hours.

When attacked by humans, rattlers do not linger until sundown to die (another old wives' tale). They die immediately, like any other vertebrate that has just received a squashed head. Nor will the mate of a dead snake stalk the killer until vengeance has been delivered. Except for a short period in the spring, rattlers do not have mates, preferring solitude to companionship.

Western Rattlesnake (*Crotalus viridis*)

ALIAS
Prairie Rattler (*Crotalus viridis lutosus*). Northern Pacific Rattler (*Crotalus viridis oreganus*). Hopi Rattler (*Crotalus viridis nuntius*). Grand Canyon Rattler (*Crotalus viridis abyssus*). Midget Faded Rattler (*Crotalus viridis concolor*). Arizona Black Rattler (*Crotalus viridis cerberus*).

IDENTIFICATION
1½-5 feet long, usually colored gray, tan, or greenish, with *dark, evenly spaced patches along the back and sides*. However, patterns are highly variable, and subspecies of western rattlers are generally identified by location and color.

Prairie Rattler (*Crotalus viridis lutosus*). Usually found on the Great Plains west to Colorado and New Mexico; usually gray.

Northern Pacific Rattler (*Crotalus viridis oreganus*). *The only species of rattlesnake*

Western Rattlesnake (prairie)

Western Rattlesnake

found in Oregon, Washington, Idaho, Montana, and Wyoming.

Hopi Rattler (Crotalus viridis nuntius). Typically inhabits rocky areas of Arizona.

Grand Canyon Rattler (Crotalus viridis abyssus). Distinguished *by its pink or salmon coloration; found exclusively in Arizona's Grand Canyon.*

Midget Faded Rattler (Crotalus viridis concolor). Inhabits the slickrock country of Colorado and Utah; small, grayish-tan, and *nearly devoid of any back pattern.*

Arizona Black Rattler (Crotalus viridis cerberus). *Colored black or dark olive;* inhabits western New Mexico and eastern Arizona.

FOOD
Small mammals, insects, lizards, birds, eggs, frogs.

ENEMIES
Predacious birds, roadrunners, kingsnakes, and man.

STATUS
Common; western rattlesnakes are one of the most widespread venomous serpents in the world.

THINGS YOU SHOULD KNOW
Western rattlesnakes are seldom aggressive. Two subspecies, the Grand Canyon rattler and the midget faded rattler, are truly cowards, slithering beneath a handy tree or down a hole when danger approaches.

Hopi rattlesnakes are used in the legendary Hopi Indian rain dances in Arizona. The snakes are wild, captured from the surrounding area a few days before the ceremony begins, and the handlers are sometimes bitten. Scientists once thought these handlers were somehow immune to snakebite, but recently it was discovered that the fangs and venom glands are removed shortly before the dances. Unfortunately, the snakes are released afterward to slowly starve to death, since they have no means of capturing prey.

Western Diamond-Back Rattlesnake (Crotalus atrox)

ALIAS
Coontail.

IDENTIFICATION
The largest of the western rattlesnakes, 3-7 feet long. The basic body color is tan or gray with large, indistinct diamonds or hexagrams set point-to-point along the back; *the tail is barred with a series of black stripes;* the head is large and flat with a pair of light-colored stripes running diagonally from the eyes to the corners of the mouth.

HABITAT
Found below 7,000 feet in southern California, Arizona, New Mexico, Colorado, extreme southern Nevada, Texas, and Mexico. Typical habitat varies from brushy river bottom to rock-strewn hillside. Diamond-backs are occasionally observed in open desert.

FOOD
The diet consists primarily of

Western Diamond-Back Rattlesnake

Western Diamond-Back Rattlesnake

kangaroo rats and other small, nocturnal rodents; also cottontails, quail, and other small birds.

ENEMIES
Birds of prey (especially red-tailed hawks), roadrunners, kingsnakes, and man.

STATUS
Common.

THINGS YOU SHOULD KNOW
Diamond-back rattlesnakes are the snakes of legend, as commonly encountered in stories of the Old West as the Colt 45. It is the diamond-back that, according to these old yarns, will not cross a lariat coiled about a sleeping cowboy because it tickles his stomach; will crawl into the bedroll if the rope is not present; rolls himself into a hoop to chase intruders; drops from rocky ledges onto the necks of unsuspecting desert travelers.

In reality, western diamond-backs are perhaps the most aggressive venomous reptile in North America, prone to attack, not run, when confronted by an enemy. Warning rattles are usually short and may come only at the moment of strike; the bite carries an enormous amount of venom. Consequently, diamond-backs are responsible for more human deaths in the United States than any other reptile.

Black-Tailed Rattlesnake (*Crotalus molossus*)

ALIAS
Dog-Faced Rattler.

IDENTIFICATION
A medium-sized, thick-bodied reptile, 2-4½ feet long. The basic body color may be dark green, army green, or yellow. *The last few inches of the tail are always black.* The back and sides are splotched with rhomboidal patches of black or brown edged in yellow or tan; the colors tend to be bright and crisp.

HABITAT
Found from sea level to 9,000 feet, but not usually below 5,500 feet, in Arizona, New Mexico, Texas, and Mexico. Typical habitat is sunny foothill slope, high desert plateau, or mesquite forest; they are probably the most common snake found around old abandoned buildings.

FOOD
Small mammals, especially

Black-Tailed Rattlesnake

rock-dwelling mice, young rabbits, birds, and lizards.

ENEMIES
Roadrunners, birds of prey, and man. Many black-tails are struck by automobiles when they venture onto black-topped mountain highways at night to absorb heat left by the sun.

STATUS
Common.

THINGS YOU SHOULD KNOW
These large, heavy, beautifully marked reptiles are not usually aggressive, preferring to hide or run instead of fight. Unlike diamond-backs, black-tails usually rattle loudly at the approach of intruders, giving clear and unmistakable warning that they do not wish to be stepped on. Black-tail venom is one of the least potent hemotoxins of the rattlesnake family; hence their bite is seldom fatal to humans.

Black-Tailed Rattlesnake

Black-Tailed Rattlesnake

Sidewinder
(*Crotalus cerastes*)

ALIAS
Horned Rattler.

IDENTIFICATION
A small, lightly-colored rattle-snake, seldom exceeding 2 feet in length. The basic body color is tan or light gray, splotched with many dark patches on the back and sides. *There is a distinctive, triangular horn above each eye.* The sidewinder's movement is unique; lateral loops of the body are thrown forward, and using the chin as a pivot, the snake pulls itself in a sideways direction.

HABITAT
Strictly nocturnal desert snakes, sidewinders are found in low, brushy or sandy areas in California, Nevada, Utah, Arizona, and Mexico. Undocumented sightings have been reported in New Mexico and Texas. Sidewinders quite often inhabit desert areas totally devoid of cover or water, burying themselves in sand as a

Sidewinder

protection against the sun.

FOOD
Small mice, rats, and some insects.

ENEMIES
Few natural predators; mainly owls and roadrunners.

STATUS
Uncommon.

THINGS YOU SHOULD KNOW
Once thought to be eyeshades against bright sunlight, a sidewinder's horns actually serve a far more important purpose. Since sidewinders often hunt rodents underground where vision is unnecessary, the horns, when bumped by a burrow wall, roof, or projecting root, fold down automatically to protect the eyes from possible laceration.

Rock Rattlesnake (*Crotalus lepidus*)

ALIAS
Green Rattlesnake, Pink Rattlesnake, Green Rock Rattlesnake.

IDENTIFICATION
A small snake, less than 25 inches long; the coloration is green or greenish-gray with *jagged brown or black bars encircling the body every few inches*. The rattles are small and generally few in number; the warning rattle may be difficult to hear. The tail tip is usually yellowish; the head is triangular but rounded.

HABITAT
Found in Arizona, New Mexico, Texas, and northern Mexico to 10,000 feet in elevation; more common at higher altitudes. Typical habitat is a boulder-strewn or brush-covered western slope near water. In some states rock rattlers are known as "mountaineer's rattlers," since climbers often discover them on mountain peaks.

FOOD
Lizards, mice, frogs, tadpoles.

ENEMIES
Birds of prey. Since their habitat is usually rugged, man and land carnivores are not serious predators.

STATUS
Rare.

THINGS YOU SHOULD KNOW
Luckily, since its venom is probably the most potent of any rattlesnake, this little serpent is not aggressive, preferring to remain hidden unless stepped on. Charles E. Shaw and Sheldon Campbell write in *Snakes of the American West* that not a single human death has ever been recorded from a rock rattlesnake's bite.

Rock Rattlesnake

Mojave Rattlesnake
(*Crotalus scutulatus*)

ALIAS
Desert Diamond Rattlesnake, Mojave Diamond Rattlesnake.

IDENTIFICATION
A medium-sized greenish or yellowish rattlesnake, 2-4½ feet long. *The back markings are perfect, uniform, dark brown diamonds, outlined in white or yellow.* The tail tip is banded by a series of narrow, indistinct, dark stripes. A dark stripe extends from the eye to the lower mandible.

HABITAT
Found from sea level to 8,000 feet in southern California, southern Nevada, and all of eastern Arizona. Typical habitat is open desert with little or no vegetation, or high, open grassland.

FOOD
Desert-dwelling rodents, rabbits, and birds.

ENEMIES
Kingsnakes, birds of prey, roadrunners.

Mojave Rattlesnake

STATUS
Uncommon.

THINGS YOU SHOULD KNOW
Mojave rattlers are quick to strike but usually coil and give plenty of warning at the approach of an intruder. Their venom, however, contains both neurotoxic and hemotoxic substances, and must be treated differently than ordinary snakebite.

11/ LIZARDS

Horned Lizard
(Phrynosoma)

ALIAS
Horned Toad, Horny Toad.

IDENTIFICATION
The most easily recognizable of any American lizard; 1-6 inches long, resembling a miniature dinosaur. *The body is wide and flat with an assembly of thick, sharp spines along the head, sides, and tail.* The color may vary from white through brown and gray; the back pattern is generally splotched with darker colors. The tail is wide, short, and usually about half as long as the body.

HABITAT
Found in all western states and Mexico from sea level to 9,500 feet. The horned lizard has no typical habitat; it may be found anywhere, but especially in sandy or rocky soil and usually in a moderate climate. Its den is a burrow or cavity beneath a rock.

FOOD
Horned lizards are ant eaters,

Horned Lizard

and a single one may consume literally thousands of ants each month. They also eat crickets, worms, snails, and beetles.

ENEMIES
Because of their formidable array of protective spines, horned lizards have few natural predators except the western collared lizard.

STATUS
Common.

THINGS YOU SHOULD KNOW
Horned lizards are oddities, unlike any other lizard. Besides their unusual shape, they have the unique ability to squirt blood from their eyes up to 4 feet when frightened or shedding skin. They also change color, usually in conjunction with daily temperature changes. On cool mornings and evenings, their colors will generally darken for total heat absorption, gradually changing to lighter, more reflective shades during warmer hours. And, when frightened or injured, horned lizards often play dead until their attacker retreats.

Gila Monster
(Heloderma suspectum)

ALIAS
Beaded Lizard.

IDENTIFICATION
A large, chubby, cylindrical lizard, 15-18 inches long, with a fat, heavy, blunt tail. Its colors may vary from brown on yellow to black on orange; *the body has a beaded appearance*; the tail is usually ringed with wide, dark bands.

HABITAT
Found mainly in Arizona and New Mexico with occasional sightings in southern Nevada, Utah, southeastern New Mexico, Arkansas, Texas, and Kansas. Typical habitat is desert, usually near cactus or other spiny cover. In Arizona and Mexico Gila monsters inhabit saguaro forests. Burrow dwellers, Gila monsters often commandeer the holes of small desert mammals. They are nocturnal.

FOOD
Very little is known about the feeding habits of these big desert lizards, but according to the herpetologist Hobart Smith, they are primarily egg eaters, probably stealing eggs from the nests of ground-laying birds. On occasion, they have also been known to consume small lizards.

ENEMIES
Man.

STATUS
Because of their enormous size and undeserved reputation for aggressiveness, Gila monsters have never been common; they are usually destroyed wherever found, if for no other reason than human uncertainty. They are presently considered rare throughout their range and protected by state law in Arizona.

THINGS YOU SHOULD KNOW
The Gila (pronounced "heela") monster is the only poisonous lizard found in the United States and one of three in the entire world. The others are the Mexican Gila monster, a close relative of the United States species, and a rare jungle lizard of Borneo. Venom is manufactured and stored in glands beneath the lower jaw, but the animals have no fangs. To take effect, the toxin must seep into wounds caused by the animal's teeth. Consequently, Gila monsters must hang onto their victim for at least a short while. They do not, however, have to turn onto their back. Tests sponsored by a national sporting magazine found that the lizards snap their heads violently from side to side or grind their teeth in order to move the toxin into a wound. The venom is a neurotoxin, affecting the nervous system and respiratory organs. However, no human death has been recorded as a direct result of a Gila monster bite. If bitten (a rare occurrence in itself), most humans are able to pry the animal loose before its venom enters the wound.

Gila Monster

Western Collared Lizard (*Crotaphytus collaris*)

ALIAS
Mountain Boomer.

IDENTIFICATION
A large, conspicuous lizard, 10 inches long; the body is wide, and the head triangular. The basic color is straw tinged with orange (colors may vary with location); there are twin sets of solid black stripes across the shoulders and gray, horizontal stripes bordered with white or blue spots across the back. The legs are dark gray.

HABITAT
Found from New Mexico west to California and from Colorado west to Oregon. Typical habitat is sandy or rocky desert, blanketed with brush and scrub. Dens are generally beneath large rocks or in shallow burrows. This lizard is most commonly observed sunning itself on a fence post or large rock.

FOOD
Horned and other small lizards, insects, and some vegetation,

usually wildflowers.

ENEMIES
Large snakes, birds of prey.

STATUS
Common.

THINGS YOU SHOULD KNOW
In an impressive show of bravado, a collared lizard when cornered will open its large, pink mouth wide, bare a row of jagged lower teeth, spread its neck, and hiss threateningly. If that doesn't drive the intruder away, the lizard will flee, moving at unbelievable speeds *on its hind legs only*.

Western Collared Lizard

Chuckwalla
(Sauromalus obesus)

IDENTIFICATION
The largest nonvenomous lizard in the United States, 14-16 inches long and up to 3½ inches wide. The basic body color is yellowish-orange, splotched with black or brownish-red. The head is wide and triangular with a large fold of skin (neck fold) just behind the ears. The legs are thick, and the toes long and slender.

HABITAT
Found below 4,000 feet in southern California, Arizona, Nevada, Utah, and Mexico. Typical habitat is rock pile or lava bed.

FOOD
Herbivorous; leaves, flowers, small succulent plants, wild fruits, and grass.

ENEMIES
In many parts of Mexico, the chuckwalla is considered a delicacy and hunted for food.

Chuckwalla

Natural enemies are predator birds.

STATUS
Uncommon.

THINGS YOU SHOULD KNOW
Disturbed chuckwallas exhibit a peculiar defensive reaction, literally blowing themselves up like balloons. According to the herpetologist G. W. Salt, they accomplish this feat by repeatedly swallowing mouthfuls of air, and then forcing it down the trachea with the tongue.

Because of their beaded appearance, these big lizards may resemble Gila monsters. However, chuckwallas seldom bite even if handled, and they carry no venom.

Like all lizards, chuckwallas are dependent on existing heat to control their body temperature. They have the ability to change color from dark to light or vice versa in order to reflect or absorb heat and light from the sun.

GLOSSARY OF ANIMAL TRACKS

Animal tracks are approximately ⅓ actual size.

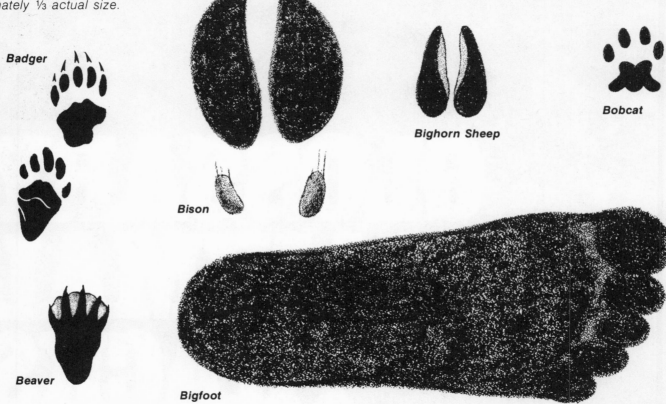

Badger

Beaver

Bison

Bighorn Sheep

Bobcat

Bigfoot

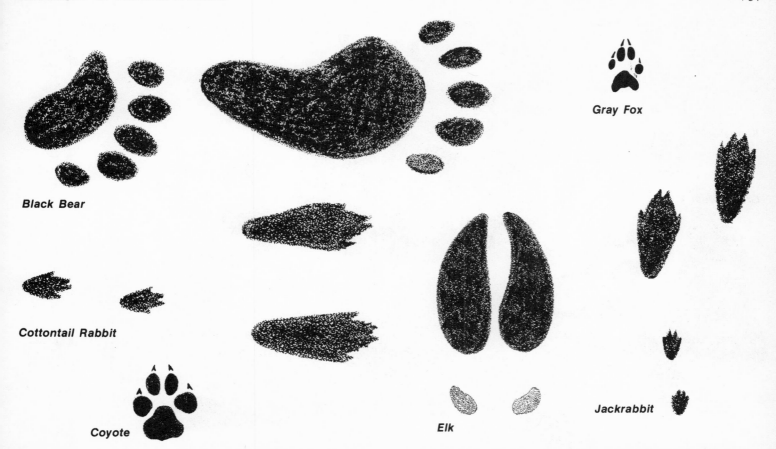

Black Bear

Gray Fox

Cottontail Rabbit

Coyote

Elk

Jackrabbit

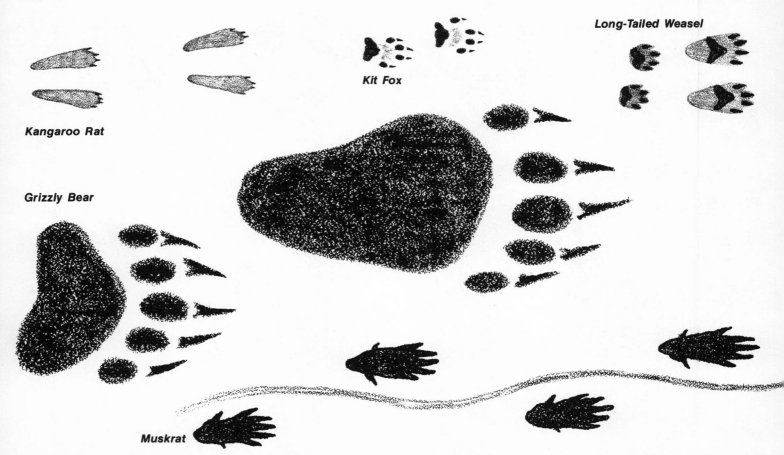

Long-Tailed Weasel

Kit Fox

Kangaroo Rat

Grizzly Bear

Muskrat

GLOSSARY OF ANIMAL TRACKS

Marmot

Mountain Goat

Mountain Lion

Mule Deer

Moose

Opossum

Peccary

Porcupine

Prairie Dog

Raccoon

Roadrunner

Turkey

Pronghorn

Red Fox

Striped Skunk

Quail

River Otter

Spotted Skunk

Wolf

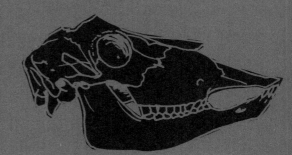

GLOSSARY
OF ANIMAL
SKULLS

MARSUPIALS

Drawings are not to scale.

Opossum

RODENTS

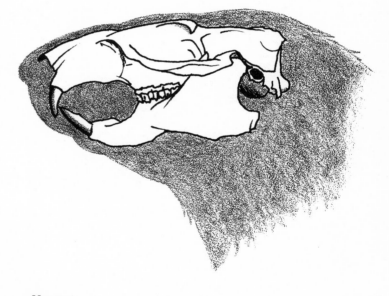

Marmot

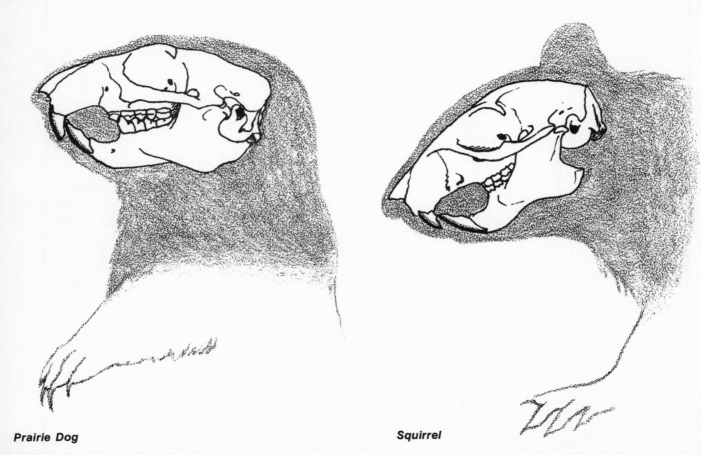

Prairie Dog

Squirrel

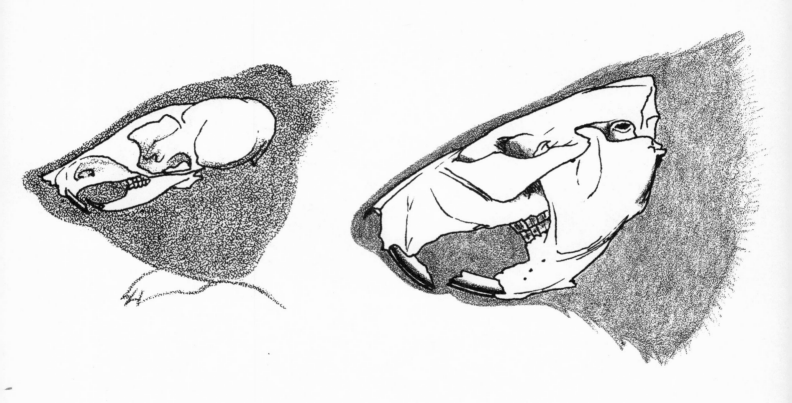

Kangaroo Rat

Beaver

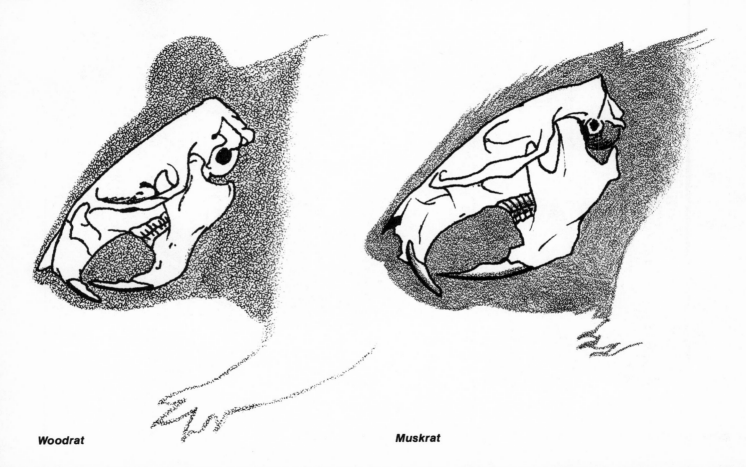

Woodrat

Muskrat

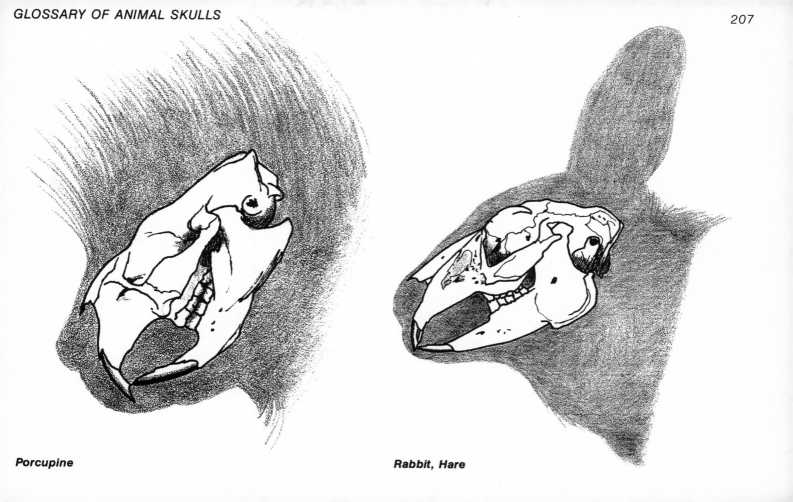

Porcupine

Rabbit, Hare

CARNIVORES

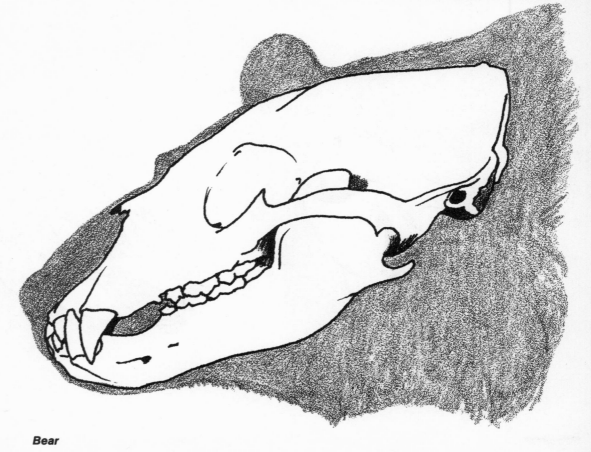

Bear

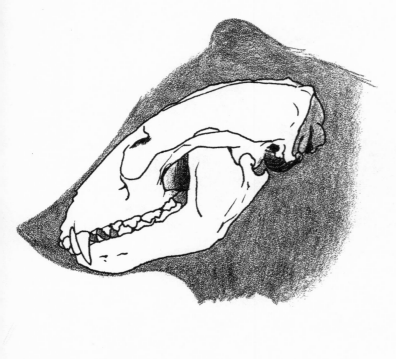

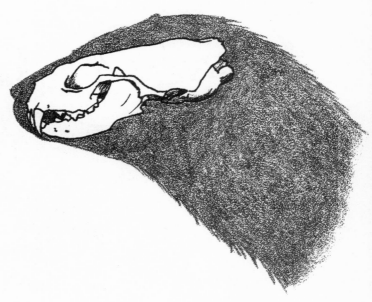

Raccoon

Weasel

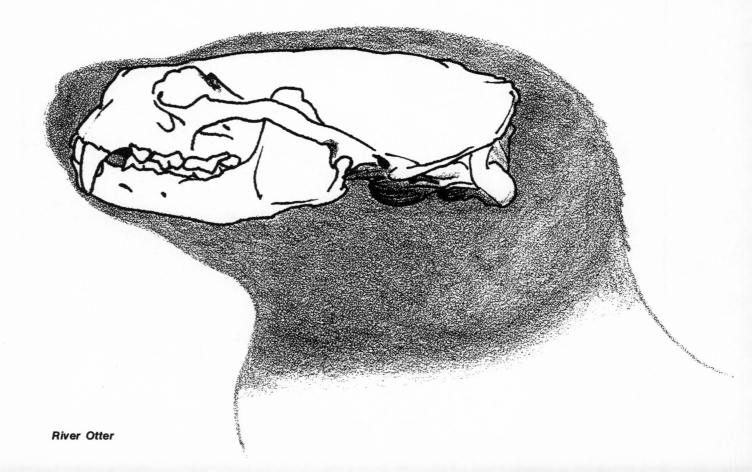

River Otter

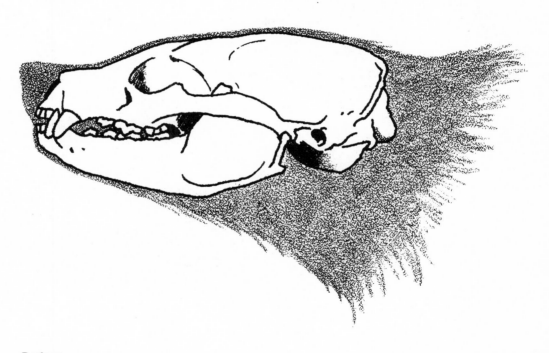

Badger

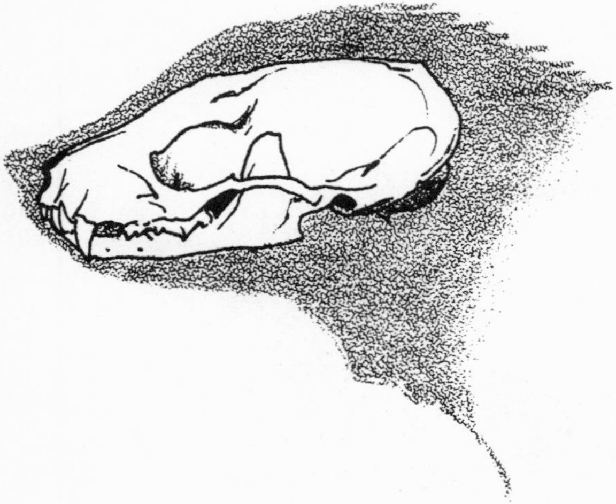

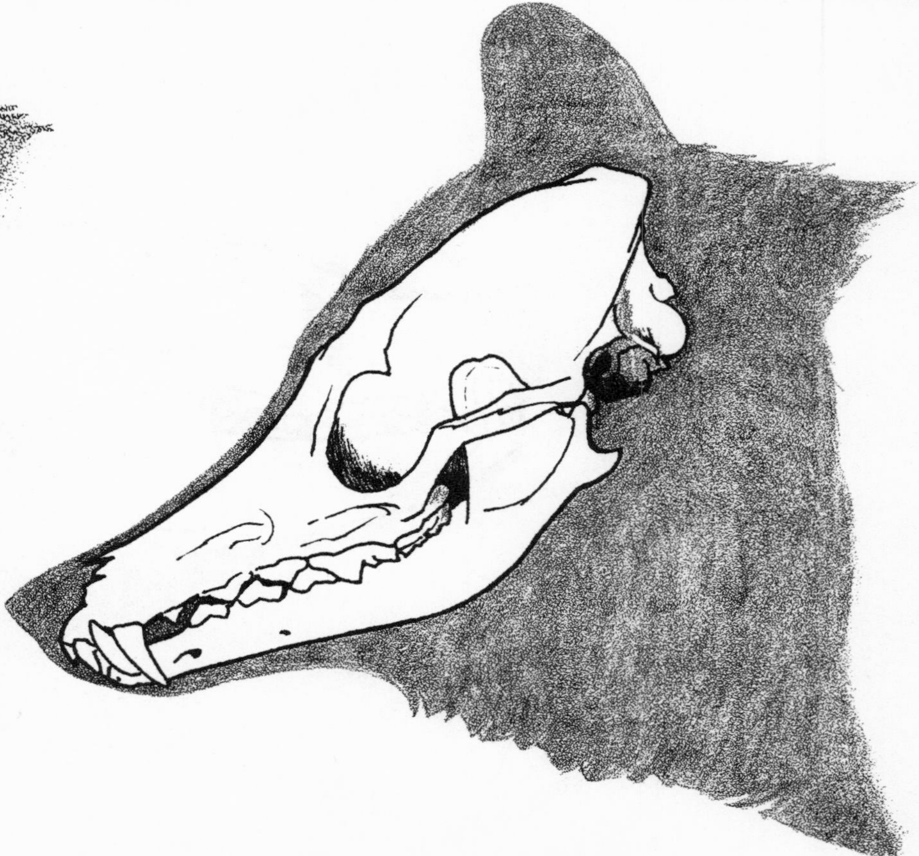

Skunk

Dog (Coyote)

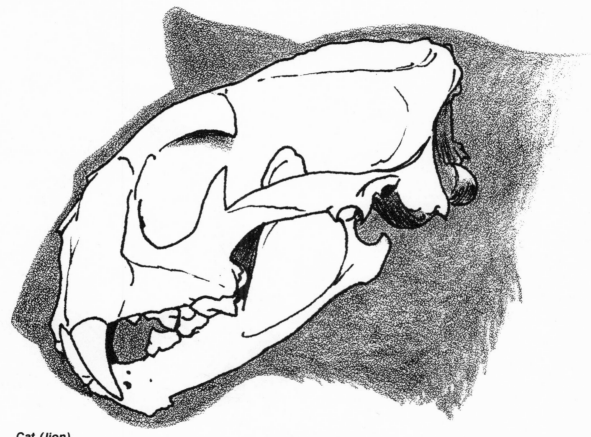

Cat (lion)

HOOFED MAMMALS (even-toed)

Peccary

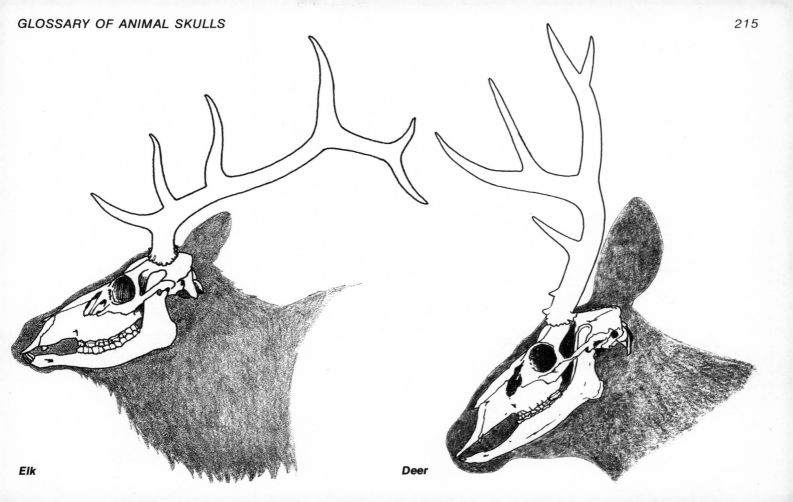

Elk

Deer

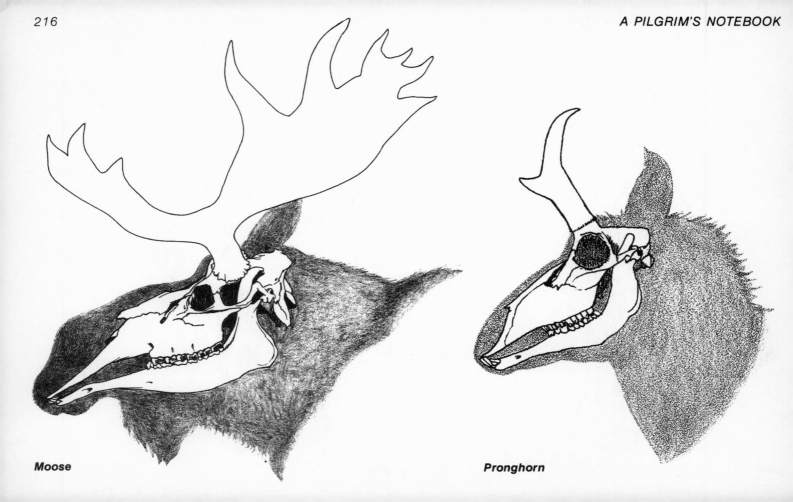

Moose

Pronghorn

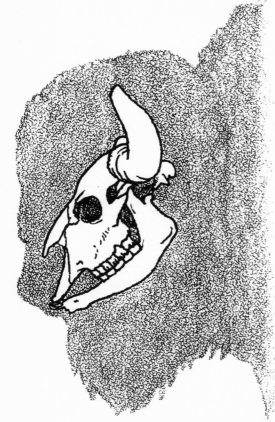

Bison

Mountain Goat

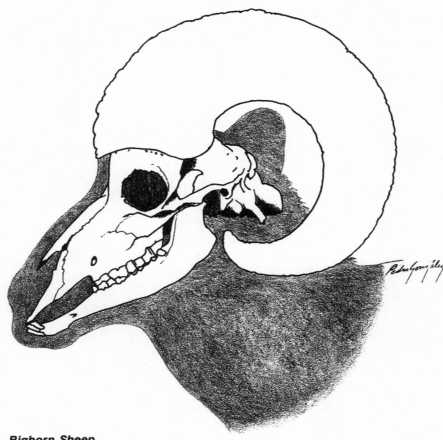

Bighorn Sheep

Threatened or Endangered Species

MAMMALS

Bat, Hawaiian Hoary (Hawaii)
Bat, Indiana (USA)
Bear, Brown (USA)
Bear, Brown (Grizzly) (Mexico)
Bison, Wood (Canada)
Bobcat (Mexico)
Cougar, Eastern (USA)
Deer, Cedros Island Mule (Mexico)
Deer, Columbian Whitetail (USA)
Deer, Key (USA)
Ferret, Black-Footed (USA)
Fox, Northern Kit (USA)
Fox, San Joaquin Kit (USA)
Jaguarundi (Mexico)
Manatee, West Indian (USA)
Mouse, Salt Marsh Harvest (USA)
Otter, Southern Sea (USA)
Prairie Dog, Mexican (Mexico)
Prairie Dog, Utah (USA)
Pronghorn, Peninsular (Mexico)
Pronghorn, Sonoran (USA, Mexico)
Rabbit, Volcano (Mexico)
Rat, Morro Bay Kangaroo (USA)
Wolf, Eastern Timber (USA)
Wolf, Gray (USA)
Wolf, Mexican (Mexico)
Wolf, Northern Rocky Mountain (USA)
Wolf, Red (USA)

BIRDS

Akepa, Hawaii (Hawaii)
Akepa, Maui (Hawaii)
Akialoa, Kauai (Hawaii)
Akiapolaau (Hawaii)
Condor, California (USA)
Coot, Hawaiian (Hawaii)
Crane, Mississippi Sandhill (USA)
Crane, Whooping (USA)
Creeper, Hawaiian (Hawaii)
Creeper, Molokai (Hawaii)
Creeper, Oahu (Hawaii)
Crow, Hawaiian (Hawaii)
Curlew, Eskimo (entire North America)
Duck, Hawaiian (Hawaii)
Duck, Mexican (USA, Mexico)
Eagle, Harpy (Mexico)
Eagle, Southern Bald (USA)
Falcon, Peregrine (entire North America)
Finch, Laysan and Nihoa (Hawaii)
Gallinule, Hawaiian (Hawaii)
Goose, Aleutian (USA)
Goose, Hawaiian (Hawaii)
Grackle, Slender-Billed (Mexico)
Hawk, Hawaiian (Hawaii)
Honeycreeper, Crested (Hawaii)
Kite, Florida Everglade (USA)
Millerbird, Nihoa (Hawaii)
Nukupuus, Kauai (Hawaii)
Oo, Kauai (Hawaii)
Ou (Hawaii)
Palila (Hawaii)
Parrot, Thick-Billed (USA, Mexico)
Parrotbill, Maui (Hawaii)
Pelican, Brown (USA, Mexico)
Poo-uli (Hawaii)
Prairie Chicken, Attwater's (USA)
Quail, Masked Bobwhite (USA)
Quail, Montezuma (Mexico)
Rail, California Clapper (USA)
Rail, Light-Footed Clapper (USA, Mexico)
Rail, Yuma Clapper (USA, Mexico)
Shearwater, Newell's Manx (Hawaii)
Sparrow, Cape Sable (USA)
Sparrow, Dusky Seaside (USA)
Sparrow, Santa Barbara (USA)
Stilt, Hawaiian (Hawaii)
Tern, California Least (USA, Mexico)
Thrush, Large Kauai (Hawaii)
Thrush, Molokai (Hawaii)
Thrush, Small Kauai (Hawaii)
Warbler, Bachman's (USA)
Warbler, Kirtland's (USA)
Woodpecker, Imperial (Mexico)
Woodpecker, Ivory-Billed (USA)

REPTILES

Alligator, American (USA)
Crocodile, American (USA)
Lizard, Blunt-Nosed Leopard (USA)
Snake, San Francisco Garter (USA)
Turtle, Aquatic Box (Mexico)
Turtle, Atlantic Ridley (Mexico)
Turtle, Softshell (Mexico)

Bibliography

Allen, Arthur A. *The Book of Bird Life*. Van Nostrand, Princeton, New Jersey, 1961.

Austin, Oliver L., Jr. *Water and Marsh Birds of the World*. Golden Press, New York, 1961.

Bailey, V. "Old and New Horns of the Prong-Horned Antelope," *Journal of Mammalogy*, 1920.

Barker, Will. *Familiar Animals of America*. Harper and Row, New York, 1951.

Bavin, Bob. "The Talking Cats," *New Mexico Wildlife*, Nov.-Dec., 1976.

Bent, Arthur Cleveland. Life Histories of North American Birds of Prey, parts 1, 2. Dover Publications, New York, 1937.

Bent, Arthur Cleveland. *Life Histories of North American Birds of Prey*, parts 1, 2. cations, New York, 1962.

Booth, Ernest Sheldon. *Birds of the West*. Stanford University Press, Stanford, California, 1950.

Caras, Roger A. *North American Mammals*. Galahad Books, New York, 1967.

Cahalane, Victor H. *Mammals of North America*. MacMillan, New York, 1947.

Collins, Henry Hill, Jr. *Complete Field Guide to American Wildlife*. Harper and Row, New York, 1959.

Cook, D. B. "History of a Beaver Colony," *Journal of Mammalogy*, 1943.

Costello, David F. *The Desert World*. Crowell, New York, 1972.

Ditmars, Raymond L. *North American Snakes*. Doubleday, New York, 1939.

Ditmars, Raymond L. *Snakes of the World*. MacMillan, New York, 1931.

Dodge, Natt N. *Poisonous Dwellers of the Desert*. 1972.

Edelbrock, Joyce. "Sea Otter," *National Wildlife*, Aug.-Sept., 1974.

Felix, Jiri. *Sea and Coastal Birds*. Octopus Books, London, 1975.

Findley, James S., and Arthur H. Harris. *Mammals of New Mexico*. University of New Mexico Press, Albuquerque, 1975.

Goodyear, Jim. "Battle for the Bighorn," *Colorado Outdoors*, Nov.-Dec., 1976.

Grossman, Mary Louise, and John Hamlet. *Birds of Prey of the World*. Clarkson N. Potter, 1964.

Hartman, J. E. "The Unfoxiest Fox," *National Wildlife*, Aug.-Sept., 1972.

Hopf, Alice L. *Wild Cousins of the Dog*. G. P. Putnam's Sons, New York, 1973.

Hornocker, Maurice. "Cougars Up Close," *National Wildlife*, Oct.-Nov., 1976.

Kauffeld, Carl. *Snakes: The Keeper and the Kept*. Doubleday, Garden City, New York, 1969.

Kaufmann, John. "Soaring Free Again," *National Wildlife*, Feb.-March, 1976.

Ligon, Stokley. *New Mexico Birds and Where to Find Them*. University of New Mexico Press, Albuquerque, 1961.

Line, Les. "Barns Are for Owls," *National Wildlife*, Dec.-Jan., 1975.

Lockley, Ronald M. *Animal Navigation*. Hart Publishing, New York, 1967.

Matthews, L. Harrison. *The Life of Mammals*. Universal Books, New York, 1971.

Murie, Adolph. *The Wolves of Mount McKinley*. U.S. Government Printing Office, Washington, D.C., 1941.

National Geographic Society. *Wild Animals of North America*. National Geographic Society, Washington, D.C., 1960.

Olin, George. *Mammals of the Southwest Desert*. U.S. Department of the Interior, 1954.

Palmer, E. Laurence. *Palmer's Fieldbook of Mammals*. Dutton, New York, 1957.

Palmer, Ralph S. *The Mammal Guide*. Doubleday, Garden City, New York, 1954.

Peterson, Roger Tory. *A Field Guide to Western Birds*. Houghton Mifflin, Boston, 1941.

Reiger, George. "The War on Predators," *National Wildlife*, June-July, 1974.

Riley, Laura. "Tiny Terror," *National Wildlife*, Aug.-Sept., 1975.

Russell, Andy. *Grizzly Country*. Knopf, New York, 1967.

Ryden, Hope. *America's Last Wild Horses*. Dutton, New York, 1970.

Scott, Jack Denton. "I Find Skunks a Delight," *National Wildlife*, June-July, 1975.

Scott, Jack Denton. "The National Symbol That Almost Was," *National Wildlife*, Oct.-Nov., 1972.

Scott, Jack Denton. "No One Badgers the Badger," *National Wildlife*, Feb.-Mar., 1971.

Seaton, Ernest Thompson. *Animal Tracks and Hunter Signs*. Doubleday, Garden City, New York, 1925.

Seaton, Ernest Thompson. *Life Histories of Northern Animals*. Doubleday, 1927.

Shaw, Charles E., and Sheldon Campbell. *Snakes of the American West*. Knopf, New York, 1974.

Smith, Hobart M. *Handbook of Lizards*. Cornell University Press, Ithaca, New York, 1946.

U.S. Department of Agriculture. *Cavity Nesting Birds of Arizona and New Mexico Forests*. April, 1975.

U.S. Department of Agriculture. *Endangered and Unique Fish and Wildlife of Southwestern National Forests*. 1975.

U.S. Department of the Interior. *The American Buffalo*. Conservation Note No. 12. Feb., 1971.

U.S. Department of the Interior. *The Bald Eagle*. Conservation Note No. 20. 1969.

U.S. Department of the Interior. *Desert Bighorn Sheep*. Conservation Note No. 19.

U.S. Department of the Interior. *Federal Register*, Vol. 41, No. 208.

U.S. Department of the Interior. *A Report on Endangered Wildlife*. Resource Publication No. 69.

U.S. Department of the Interior. *United States List of Endangered Fauna*. May, 1974.

U.S. Department of the Interior. *Waterfowl Tomorrow*. 1964.

U.S. Department of the Interior, Fish and Wildlife Service. *Ducks at a Distance*.

Wormer, Joe Van. *The World of the Canada Goose*. Lippincott, Philadelphia, 1968.

Wormer, Joe Van. *The World of the Pronghorn*. Lippincott, Philadelphia, 1969.

Notes